Burnout

Hayden Plunkett

Table of Contents

PART ONE: HOT SEAT

PART TWO: SHOCK AND AWE

PART THREE: THE BIRD CAGE

PART FOUR: ANTEROGRADE

PART ONE

HOT SEAT

Chapter One

Edgar

"Eternity scares the hell out of me."

"I can turn from it, I can ignore it, but the fear never really goes away. It always comes creeping back, seeping from the darkness, and grinning with those gnarled, yellow teeth. Shouting, in the depths of the night: 'Leave me, Edgar, you beast! Leave me!' I named him. That makes it easier, somehow."

"It has been difficult to admit this fear, even to myself. As if speaking it aloud, or even putting it onto paper, will somehow summon him- that dreadful Edgar- back into this world."

"Maybe it's because I am a writer. I was born a writer; I have always known it. And with that knowledge, a curse: an inherent understanding that all stories, good or bad, have a natural conclusion. At one point or another, they all burn out."

"This may come as a surprise to you, but I believe in the afterlife. I believe in Heaven, and I believe in Hell. Clouds and the golden gates and a shining sun forever. Fire, and the eternal gnashing of teeth. For me, both options are equally unappealing. What worries me, more than anything is the 'forever' part."

"Heaven and Hell. Eternity and… eventual emptiness. These dichotomies weigh upon me at every waking moment."

Chapter Two

Feng Shui

"That was deep, man."

"Yeah, you went full monologue there, it was great."

Maybe I should explain. You see, that last little spiel about eternity? That was part of a drinking game. The way it works, everyone goes one round in the "Hot Seat," meaning no question is off limits. Anyone can ask you anything, and it is in your best interest to answer every question. If you *do* refuse to answer a question, you have to take a shot. Simple, right?

"*What is your greatest fear?*" That was the one they came up with, right off the bat. A bit intimate for a first impression, but I didn't mind. Tonight, I am an entertainer, first and foremost. And, in that respect, tonight has been a success; I seem to have piqued the interest of the room. Everyone, that is, except for the girl in the corner, with the frazzled hair, and the dark, swooping circles beneath her eyes. *She's beautiful, though. Behind all of that, there's something beautiful about her.*

"That Edgar shit gave me goosebumps, dude. The guy sounds absolutely terrifying." Oh, he is, believe me. Goosebumps, though? The guy's never given me goosebumps. The only thing he brings to the table is a dull, throbbing ache in my stomach, like a darkened void, draining away the light.

You know who gives me goosebumps? The girl in the corner, with the frazzled hair- Daisy, I believe that's her name. There is an energy about her; a balance in the room as her gaze lands upon me, like a river, slithering out from the mountains, wrapping around a sweltering fire, and protecting the Earth from its deathly grasp.

The withered, leather couch squeals as I lean forward. "Well, I'm glad you enjoyed it. Sure, it was a bit melodramatic, but, as a writer, I crave that type of stuff. It's not often that I actually get to *speak* on something like that, you know?" Daisy's gaze has transformed into a glare. It is unnerving and exhilarating at the same time, like a beating of drums, warning of the war to come.

A war of water and fire.

A Feng Shui to keep the peace.

Alexa- she's the one who invited me here, and one of two names that I remember- chimes in. "Alright, Forrest, that's eight seconds on the clock. You ready for the next question?" A few more rules: the Hot Seat lasts 30 seconds. Not a *real* 30 seconds, but 30 seconds of answering. Every answer has a maximum of eight seconds on the clock. You can go over, but it doesn't add to your time.

"I hope you have something special up your sleeve because it's going to take a lot more to get me drinking. I'm an open book." Daisy's leg begins to tremble. There is a dull, rhythmic thumping. *The war drums, they are getting louder.*

"Daisy, is everything alright?"

"Yeah, I'm okay, it's just…" There is no holding it back. What was once a storm pours out over the river bank. White, roaring rapids, spill onto the charring earth, flowing through the crackling wildfire. "You know, that's bullshit man! It's just bullshit!"

A whirlwind of shattered fragments- shards of chaos and flame- burn out within my soul, extinguished by the flood. "What's bullshit, exactly?" A menacing grin rises like smoke upon my face.

"I mean, it's like you think life is just some sort of… *novel!* Just a story some guy cracked up for a few extra bucks." Strangely enough, *that* is what I am afraid of. *That* is Edgar. He is the chilling realization- sprung to life in those awful, lonely nights- that life will go on and on, like a series whose author, as a betrayal to his art, has ignored its natural conclusion, and kept it alive for the sole purpose of sustaining his bank account.

But I have no intention of correcting her.

"Well, newsflash, asshole! You know what's worse than eternity? When you turn to that final page, hoping for more, and there is nothing. A darkened, meaningless void... and there is nothing you can do about it! Isn't that more terrifying than your fucking *Edgar?!*" Scorched earth turns to scorched mud, oozing from beneath the lingering flames. The river pulls away; she doesn't bother waiting for a response. She storms out from her corner, knocking a drink over as she cuts past the table. Thunderous, booming stomps fill the hallway, leading to her room. She slams the door behind her.

Alexa secures the fallen glass- by some miracle, the thing didn't break- while someone else rushes to the kitchen for some paper towels. "You'll have to excuse her," Alexa says, looking up from the mess, "she's going through a rough time right now."

That much, at least, was apparent. "Do you mind if I ask what?" I shake my head because I know it is intrusive. "Sorry, you don't have to. Just... maybe it would be good to know so I can avoid sensitive topics with her in the future."

"No, that's alright. She is pretty open about it." She moves back to the couch, and the other guy- "Thanks, Dylan," – the guy with dreads, Dylan, throws a mound of paper towels on the puddle of mixed drink. "I don't feel comfortable going into *too* much detail, but I will say that she is going through withdrawal symptoms right now."

"That's..." There is a searing pain inside me. It feels like a lifetime ago, but I, too, am familiar with the pain of withdrawal. "That's tough, I didn't realize." I should have guessed it earlier. "I hope she gets better soon." It's all starting to come together. The messy look, the quivering leg. I am impressed, really, that she mustered up the strength to hang out with us tonight. I am glad she did, because, otherwise... well, that would have ruined my plans.

I take a quick peek down the hallway. Two rooms, but only one of them with the door shut. *That's good, that's really good; her room adjoins the bathroom. Now I just have to wait until she comes back.*

"So, looks like we got a little off track," Dylan continues, leaving the paper towels to soak, "but... would you be up for another question?"

With Daisy gone and the war at a standstill, my role as an entertainer has once again come to the forefront. "I don't see why not. What have you got for me?"

"Well, I think it's Serena's turn for a question. Do you have a good one, Serena?"

Serena, another name to add to the list. I haven't gotten a good read on her yet. She is best friends with Alexa, since childhood, that's all I know; so her question should be interesting. She turns to me with a smile. "Yeah, I've got one. But don't worry, Forrest, it's a bit of a softball."

"Softballs, bowling balls. I really don't mind. Throw anything you've got."

"And that is the *perfect* lead into my question. You see, Forrest, you seem like a charming guy. You had other options tonight, I'm sure of it. So, I'm curious: What brought you here, tonight, out of all places?"

Chapter Three

Toucan

Serena, it seems, is a force to be reckoned with; as much as she would want you to believe it, that question was, by no means, a softball. That was a colossal, tumbling bowling ball, and she knew it.

To answer her question, let me begin by saying that I have always been a proponent of fate. I see life as a long journey down a winding path. There may be a few missteps along the way, but I believe, whatever happens, the invisible hand of fate will guide the wanderer back along the path. And that path has led me here, out of all places.

In a sense, if I were to answer her question fully, I would have to understand the mechanisms of fate. I do not claim to have that knowledge. I do, however, understand the mechanisms of my (conscious) mind. And my (conscious) mind has brought me here for one, all-important task: to regain my most prized possession.

It all started two weeks ago when I was studying in the library. I used to be very mindful of my belongings, but, over the years, I have become very trusting of my peers. I had to go to the bathroom and had no intention of bringing my backpack with me. Who would steal someone's laptop or backpack, anyways, with so many people around, watching over? I thought they would have been busy studying. Clearly, that was a mistake.

When I got back, it was all gone. My laptop, my headphones. They could probably make a decent profit off of my old watch in there, alone. I didn't care about any of that, though. What I was most worried about was my journal. Now, that may sound ridiculous, but that journal has the happenings of my life, day in and day out, for the past two years. My trials, my tribulations. My daily conversations. I had hoped that one day it would be the source of my autobiography. To me, that is more valuable than any laptop, or any watch.

I was devastated, and, for a while, I didn't know what to do with myself. I had these crazy thoughts go through my head, that maybe this was a sign from God; maybe I was not meant to be a writer.

However, the real sign from God came a few days later.

I decided to go to a different café. Rio Café; I had always wanted to try it out. It was tempting, with its lively, artsy vibe, and its vibrant paintings of toucans and jungle scenery. I always felt those toucan eyes staring into my soul, calling me inside, beckoning me towards that sweet life-force that has fueled so much of my writing. As a devotion to my routine, and my usual café, I had never listened to that persuasive, black toucan. But, this was different. With my journal gone and my future vanished, I felt a change in routine was in order.

I was going through my usual process: read for ten minutes, buy a coffee… daydream for another five, before getting to work on my novel. I was in the daydreaming phase when, suddenly, I was jolted awake by some eerie, prevailing feeling. I realized I must have been staring at this girl across the room for quite some time. I tried to turn away, but something about her had caught my attention, and I couldn't keep my eyes off of her. It took me several minutes to figure out what that was.

It was her backpack.

At first glance, it was just an average, black backpack. But, my eyes kept turning back to it, and I knew there was something up about it. I got up to go to the bathroom, and, when I passed by, I saw the label had been torn off on the bottom right corner, just as mine had been. Not only that, but there was a hole on the outside, bottom pocket, carelessly patched over with a strip of bright, blue duct tape.

This was my backpack, no doubt about it.

At first, I thought I would confront her, but that thought went out the window when I realized, on my way back from the bathroom, that she didn't have my journal on her. No, if I was going to do this, I would need to get creative. I knew, in that moment, that this would be the greatest test of my writing abilities. Sure, I can write novels, but can I write my own destiny, and get my life's work back into the palms of my hands?

I believed that I could. And yet, somewhere, deep inside, I knew there was another motivating factor behind all of this. I thought for a while it was her beauty, but I realize now it was the balance I felt when I looked at her, and those goosebumps that made their way up my arms.

If you haven't figured it out by now, that girl was Daisy.

I deliberated for a long time over my course of action. I thought I might steal something of hers, and make an exchange for my journal. Or maybe I might follow her home, and find a way to break in. These were interesting scenarios, but they weren't me. They weren't *believable.* Not for my character, at least.

This was writer's block full swing, let me tell you. *Nothing* good was coming to me. Not, at least, until the barista came up to Daisy, and started a conversation. "Daisy! How was your test today?"

"It was a little tough, but I think I did alright." She frowns. "I've got another one tomorrow. School really hasn't given me a break, lately."

"Awwhh, Daisy!" She squats down to the height of her booth and gives her a sympathetic hug. "If anyone deserves a break, it's you. But don't worry, it's coming soon enough, I can feel it." She smiles. "You left your keys at home, by the way." She pulls the keys out of her apron and places them on the table. "Maybe not the break you were looking for, but at least you'll be able to get home tonight."

"Thank you so much, that…" Her eyes well up, like a flooding river. They hug once more, for good measure. "It just means a lot. Thank you."

"I mean, it was just your keys. Anyone would have brought them."

"No, I mean for the support. It just… it means a lot. I couldn't ask for a better friend. Thank you, Alexa."

Yes, that Alexa.

Alexa, really, was the key to this whole plan. She was that glass of champagne, broken upon the bow of a new ship, that has christened so many novels, and blessed me, at the threshold of my new narrative. I stood, in that moment, on a dock of fate, with a luminous sunset melding with the blue of the Pacific.

I'm sure the Rio Toucan was looming in the distance.

Chapter Four

Pineapple

I spent the following evening developing my protagonist, as I always do before a novel or a short story. This was not your usual protagonist, however. This was *me*. *Me,* but amplified, slightly. A fun-loving guy, easy to hang around with. A good listener, with an uncanny ability to make your voice feel heard. He's extremely intuitive, and can always tell when someone is down. In these cases, he will do his absolute best to cheer you up. Which is why, when appropriate, he *always* has a smile on his face; he's more approachable that way.

Approachability, that is the key here.

He wears interesting shirts, as a catalyst for conversation. For his Rio debut, he went with a classic: a plain, regular t-shirt, with a pineapple plastered on the front. It is not his favorite in the world, but it is his most successful conversation starter. He wears attire like this to get the spotlight turned on him, and allow the world to see his charm; he is an entertainer, above all else. This is how he meets new people.

Today, it will be how he meets the barista.

There was a certain warmth, a certain kindness in her voice that was impossible to miss. "Hi, welcome to Rio, how can I help you today?" The otherwise simple phrasing sprung to life with the help of her sprightly, bubbly nature. Surely, this is a persona she puts on for work… and yet, there was an authenticity to it. In a sense, she is not much different from the protagonist: real, but exaggerated.

I put on a wide, genial grin. "Well, I am in desperate need of some coffee, but I am really open to anything. I'm new here, so… I don't know, what would you recommend?" I could almost feel my eyes glowing- a technique I had practiced in the mirror the night before- and I believe she felt it, too. She turned away, simpering. She may as well have been staring into the sun.

"Well," she said, turning back to me, "if you are looking for coffee, I would recommend the flat white, that is my personal favorite. But, we also have a variety of smoothie options, if you are interested in that." Her eyes found their way to the pineapple, like a vulture, spotting its prey. "I like your shirt, by the way."

I chuckled, slightly; everything, it seemed, was going according to plan. "Thank you. I thought it worked well with the whole jungle theme you have here."

"Well, *yeah,* it fits perfectly!" she exclaimed with childish glee, motioning towards the pineapple painted on the wall.

"Perfectly!" I repeated cheerily, acting as an echo chamber. This was more of an excited, knee-jerk reaction than anything. Were things really running this smoothly? Was I, truly, the author of my own fate?

The toucan's hypnotic eyes leered at me from the back wall. The bird stood at a fascinating angle; in my head, he was perched, like royalty, on Alexa's shoulder. "Speaking of pineapples, we *do* have a pineapple smoothie- it's probably our most popular option- if you want to go all out on the pineapple theme today."

And so, I did. And the next day, as well. I was tempted to order coffee- I needed it, I truly did- but I went with the pineapple, as a sign that she was still on my mind. On the third day, I went back to coffee.

Every day, a new, interesting shirt. Every day, a new, flirtatious conversation. An intricate, floral design, but only on the sleeves. A Hawaiian, with coconuts scattered throughout. And, on the third day- I made this purchase, specifically, with the café in mind- a toucan, perched on a tree, staring into the sunset.

On the third day, someone else took my order. This was no accident; Alexa saw me approaching and asked to switch places with her coworker. My mind went wild with theories as to what I had done wrong. For a moment, I was worried she thought I was leading her on. This would not be a ridiculous assessment; we had been flirting for days, now, and I had not made a move. However, this was, by no means, the case. While I may have been using her for the journal, I was quite enamored by her, and her warmth. It was on this third day, in fact, that I had planned to ask her out.

When I went to order, I could tell she was listening. My words brought her dishwashing to a standstill, and I could see those green, emerald eyes peering out from her peripherals. She tried to cover it up, but she was smiling, too. A faint, delicate smile, but it was there, and it was visible. *Maybe this is a good sign, after all.*

I ordered a coffee. I needed it.

I thought long and hard on the subject and was willing to admit defeat. What had I seen in that smile, in those emerald eyes, anyway? It was all just a figment of the imagination.

And yet, by the time I finished my coffee, a fresh cup of blended pineapple had found its way to my table. Several orange, citrus droplets splattered across her apron. “Do you think I would let you get away without a pineapple smoothie?” she quipped. “Come on, I know it’s your favorite.” That warm, endearing smile. “It’s on me, don’t worry.”

“That’s… that’s, uh…” I was at a loss for words. “That’s really nice of you. Thank you, Alexa.”

She was smirking, now, as if she had me in her corner. “You can make it up to me by coming to my party tonight. It’s at my place, 10 o’clock.” Little did she know, I was *hoping* to be cornered. Little did she know, this was my *design,* sprung to life.

Had I really done it?

I’m not entirely sure what was said after that; I went into an almost comatose, autopilot state. All I know is that there was an exchange of numbers, an exchange of addresses, and…

Well, yes, I had done it.

I was a better writer than I could have ever imagined.

Chapter Five

Half-Truths

The party was just like any other in our festive, college town. Pulsing music with mesmerizing lights, swaying from the balcony. The DJ huddled in the corner. The manic crowd pinned around him in a muddled, anarchic fashion. The sound of waves crashing below the bluffs, whispering to those strangers on the ledge, staring into the black horizon.

Generally, nights like these end with some girl, craving an invitation to that world beneath the sheets. They end with me, explaining that my days in that world have been put on hold. They end, alone, in agonizing contemplation, wondering if this festive, college beach town was meant for me, after all.

I had other plans tonight.

The crowd died after midnight. I was invited inside to play drinking games, as I had expected.

"What brought you here, tonight, out of all places?"

If I were to answer that question honestly, my plans would be ruined. *A half-truth, that is the only solution here.* A bowling ball, just as I told you, but not for the reasons Serena thought. It was clear, to me at least, that Serena was playing the role of wing-woman. She heard about our flirtations and knew Alexa had invited me here. Now, she wanted to hear my side of it. Maybe, just maybe, she could get me to admit my feelings for Alexa. *Alexa brought me here tonight, out of all places.*

As hard as it is for me to admit it, I believe I have lost those feelings. They were there, for a moment, but... Let's just say, if Daisy had never been put into the equation, I feel this story would have gone very differently.

That may sound out of line. I mean, I just met the girl, right? How can I be sure there is anything there? At least, with Alexa, we have proven chemistry. That is a decent argument, sure, but there are some things in life that cannot be argued. Goosebumps, for example. There is no arguing the goosebumps. There is no arguing the balance, the Feng Shui, I feel when I look at her. That might all sound like bullshit to you, but to me? Nothing has ever felt more real.

"Here?" I jest, mocking the theatre of her question. "Here, *out of all places?!*" The room erupts in laughter, but it is a peculiar laughter. The type that is given to the witticisms of a potential employer: real,

but exaggerated. “Man, this was the absolute, dead-end, *last* place I wanted to end up tonight, *but here I am,*” I snicker, “out of *aaaaaaaaaallllllllllllll* places.” My arms get wider and wider with the extended *aaaallllllll,* and when I do, eventually, reach the limits of my wingspan, I throw myself back onto the tattered, leather couch.

An entertainer, above all else.

But now, I must dodge the bowling ball, and answer the question. Now, I must release that nasty, snarling half-truth.

“In all seriousness, I met Alexa, and we really hit it off.” It’s painful, the way she looks at me. Like an eager child, awaiting her father’s bedtime story. *I am sorry to disappoint, Alexa. These half-truths are not designed for slumber; they are designed to keep you up at night.* “When she invited me here, I jumped on that chance to get to know her better.” *There are only half-truths, here, teetering on the edge of fantasy and reality.* “I am so, *so* glad I did. And that I got the chance to meet all of you, as well. All because I wore some stupid pineapple shirt.” Alexa giggles at that one. There is a nice, tingly feeling at the sound of it, but it transcends into a throbbing, salient ache, that oozes like melting wax down my spine; I realize, now, that I am leading her on.

It kills me inside… and yet, if I want that journal, there is not much I can do about it.

Chapter Six

Forbidden

Dylan asks the next question. His eyes are a grey-ish, green-ish hue; he uses them as daggers, piercing into my soul, and searching for that one, forbidden question. *Ask it, Dylan, I dare you.* He bites his lower lip; he can't find anything, I'm sure of it, but he keeps on digging. He keeps on digging, until-

Daisy returns to the living room. Her arms are crossed, shielding herself from unwanted attention. There is a lingering silence, like a cloud of fog hanging over us. She reclaims her seat as if nothing out of the ordinary has just occurred. "Well, go on. Don't wait for me."

"I'm still thinking," he says, almost in a haze, before releasing his lower lip. "No, no… uh, scratch that, I think I got one." There is an ominous smirk laden across his face. I get an unnerving feeling at the sight of it, like something- a piece within me- must make amends, and put an end to its time in the shadows. The daggers come around again, making sure that everything is in order. That this question is, as he hopes, that one, forbidden question.

"Just ask it already," I mumble beneath my breath.

He chuckles silently; he knows he has me in his corner. "Alright Forrest, here it goes," he rises from his seat, so as to judge me from above. *"What is the worst thing you have ever done?"*

I look at him with wide, glimmering eyes. *Please take it back.* The question is everything I feared it would be. *Please take it back, Mister Dreads. Please.* That one, forbidden question… how did he find it?

In retrospect, I know how he did it. It's simple, really. We all have that one, dark secret. That secret we have vowed to never tell a soul. Some are worse than others. Some are revolting, unpleasant wrecks, while others are, largely, harmless. Whatever the case, no secret is harmless to its keeper. *"What is the worst thing you have ever done?"* For those that haven't faced it- and most, I believe, haven't- the question is a ringer for that "forbidden" category.

There are several ways I could go about this. I could tell the truth and face that night, with all its horrors. *No… no, you can't do that. Don't even joke about that.* I could serve up another one of those delicious, mouthwatering half-truths, straight out of the oven. *These half-truths are not designed for slumber; they are designed to keep you up at night.* Heck, I could go straight for the jugular, and gift my new friends with a plate of blatant falsities. I'm a writer, after all, I could make it believable.

But the thought of it, *even the thought of that answer,* sends me into a whirlwind that can only be quelled with the taste of sweet, burning liquid.

I pour the shot myself.

It trickles down my throat, sanitizing all traces of that night, long ago, which I had hoped to send into oblivion. Dylan hands me a glass of orange juice. "Chaser?" I wave him off, there is no need for that. What I need, right now, is a cleansing.

The fog sinks to the floorboards and seeps through the house in a haunting, ghoulish manner. Empty, dead stares rest upon my shoulders. There is a dreadful ambience in the room, and it is bitter to the taste.

"Next question, please."

Chapter Seven

Silver

"And… I'm only at 16 seconds." I need to move this game along; with Daisy in the ring again, I have a chance to steal my journal back, but who knows how long that will last. *It's just 14 seconds man, it's almost over. 14 seconds and everything will be back to normal.* "This has been one heck of a Hot Seat, let me tell you."

"Yeah, I'm sorry Forrest," Serena says, the first one to break from the fog, "this has been a tough round." She shrugs. "That's how the game goes, I guess." She places a hand on Alexa's shoulder. "It's your turn for a question, isn't it?"

Alexa's mind, it seems, is stuck on that last, unanswered question. I'm sure she is wondering- I'm sure they are *all* wondering- what awful, horrid thing I did, that could warrant such a response. Alexa, Dylan, and Daisy linger in that state for quite some time. *They'll come back, don't worry. Eventually, it's gonna' hit them: they, too, have dark secrets.* Secrets which may demand a shot, over honesty.

"Sorry, yes… yes, it's my turn." There is a devious humor in her eyes when she does, eventually, find her way back from that murky, creeping mist. "Don't worry, I have one prepared." Those eyes find their way to the toucan on my shirt- this seems to startle her, as if she saw that shirt several eons ago, and not this very morning- before edging their way back to *my* eyes. Those eyes which are ocean blue, but certainly not glowing as they were on that fateful day in Rio. "This one's a bit of a cliché, but it's a cliché for a reason." Those eager, warm, devious eyes. There is a chorus in the room; they seem to know what is coming. *"How many sexual partners have you had?"* The room groans in excitement.

I do welcome the change in tone, but there is a problem with the question: it is far too simple. I can't just answer with a number, that won't add any time to the clock. Time which I desperately need, if I am going to get the journal. *You'll have to stall, just a little bit. You don't know how crucial those extra seconds might be.* "Well, it depends on if you are counting third-"

"We're talking fourth base," she says candidly.

"Then… in that case… I have had," counting on my fingers, "three sexual partners."

Alexa stops the timer. 23 seconds. *Okay, I can work with that.*

The crowd seems astonished- there is a murmur making its way through the room- and I am not sure whether they think the number is too high, or too low. *Why do they care so much, anyway?* Daisy's eyes widen in a moment of realization. She points at my chest, from across the room.

"Your necklace," she says. "Show us your necklace."

She doesn't need to say it; my hands have already wrapped around the cool, metallic chain, and I pull back to reveal a silver, cross necklace. Dylan gasps, if only slightly. "What?" I query. "Do you think I'm ashamed of it or something?" There is a sadness in my voice. "Since when did this become something to be ashamed of? Anyways, I said it earlier. I believe in Heaven and Hell."

"Well, that doesn't necessarily mean you are a Christian."

"Yeah, sure, it doesn't, but-"

"That wasn't my point, Forrest," Daisy says. "I think it's beautiful, actually, as long as you're not one of those crazy fanatics. Just… not to be judgmental, but I'm curious. You are afraid of eternity, you have some terrible secret you refuse to tell us about- okay, fine, most people do- but you said you have been with three partners, so… are you just ignoring the whole premarital sex thing?"

I smile because I think I can put an end to this Hot Seat, after all. "Does that count as another question?" I retort.

"Well…"

"It's your turn anyways, Daisy. Just, count it as another question, and we can get this round over with."

"Okay, fine. That's my question. How do you justify sleeping with three partners, when you claim to be a Christian?"

This is it; this is the home stretch. "I became a Christian pretty recently, actually. Two years ago, almost to the date." Three days, actually, until the anniversary of my baptism. "The three partners that I told you about, they happened before I converted." The seven seconds pass, but there is one, final thing that I can't hold back. "That terrible little secret, the worst thing I have ever done, that was my breaking point." My hands cling to the silver cross. "That's what brought me to Christ."

Chapter Eight

Denial

My chest is the trunk of a black sedan, and my heart, its curious baggage: an abductee, hands tied, and gagged to silence. A ferocious desire to break free curbed only by the need to conserve energy. Constrained prying against the latch. Noiseless strikes against the panels. The knowledge that, to struggle too much, is to risk everything.

The plan is simple.

You're in the home stretch, you can do this. I excuse myself to the bathroom. My last visit was fairly recent, so I need an excuse. "Man, breaking the seal was a *bad* decision," I quip, before making my way down the hallway. No eyebrows raised. No reaction at all, really. *That's good, that's what you want.* There is a rush of adrenaline as I lock the door behind me, and make my way around the sink. The door- the door which leads to the bedroom- is slightly ajar; my first glimpse of the room, *Daisy's* room, spills through the crack, like a leaking faucet. *This is it, man. Author of your own destiny.*

Constrained prying against the latch.

Noiseless strikes against the panels.

There is a steady, restrained creaking as I open the door. I use my shirt as a gas-mask; there is an overwhelming aroma of perfume and vomit. I spot my backpack, with the blue tape and the torn label, cradled against the foot of her bed. I make a beeline in that direction, crouched all the while, and making sure to run on my toes.

I tear the bag open, but there are only unfamiliar notebooks. *You knew that, you idiot,* I scold myself, smacking my forehead, *you saw that in the café.* I scavenge through her bed but to no avail. No laptop, no headphones. No old watch, either.

Constrained prying aga-

Noiseless stri-

Panic sets in. There is no logic in the hunt, only haphazard spirals, and arbitrary tossing of objects. The room becomes a dizzying swirl of dim lights and dirty laundry. I have nearly given up hope-

Abort mission! Too much time, abort mission!

-when, suddenly, the cyclone steadies, and narrows in on that beautiful, leather-bound journal, resting on the nightstand.

The abductee takes a break from its scramble, allowing itself a moment of rest. A muffled sigh of relief through the dirty cloth, which blocks its airways. *This is it. We really did this, didn't we?* What follows, is more of an out of body experience than anything.

I turn for the doorway but stop to bring the journal to my chest, as a mother embraces her child.

I scroll through the pages, taking in that magnificent scent of paper and ink.

Every trial, every tribulation, for the past two years.

There are highlights, now. I never highlighted anything. *Why are there highlights?*

Noiseless strikes aga-

One of the pages is dog-eared. My mind tells me to book it out of there, but my body is frozen, my jaw is hanging, and my hands turn to the page. There is one, glaring highlight, streaked across the page. The line is jagged- piercing the line above it, and with a light kiss to the line below- but the quote is clear, both in the journal and in my memory. *There is a power in denying oneself.*

A jarring scream in the distance. *"Don't touch that, you asshole!"* Except for it is not in the distance, but in my ear. An astonished glance to my left brings me to Daisy's maddened face, with lips curling and nose crinkled in a ball of rage.

The river is now an ocean, and the fire doesn't stand a chance.

The absent pressure in my shoulder becomes an aching, searing agony.

A silver switchblade branches out of me, like an extra limb.

Drops of red come pouring out, and I collapse against the floor.

PART TWO

SHOCK AND AWE

Chapter One

Shock

My vision burns away at the edges, like a photograph, succumbing to the flicker of a match. Daisy's magnificent face, with the swooping dark, circles, and the frazzled hair, melts along my peripherals, looking down on me in a concoction of anger and shame.

"Did you fucking *stab* him?!" Alexa shouts, barreling into the room.

Daisy brings her hands to her face, gaping at the sight of her bloody palms. Her teeth chatter- like mother's china cabinet, at the first sign of an earthquake- before shutting swiftly. "He was going through my fucking journal, Lex, what was I supposed to do?"

"Uhh… I don't know. Not stab him? Ever consider that one, *Daisy?!*"

"Look, you know how important that journal was to me. I overreacted… sure… but I'm fucking *jumpy* okay?!" A mess of ash, and rising smoke.

"You can't use that excuse for every little thing, Daisy," Serena says, butting in. "What did you-" There is no need to finish the question. "Oh… oh *shit*."

"What were you doing, snooping through my journal anyways, you little shit?" Daisy snarls, crouching over me.

"Daisy, you just stabbed the guy… and *he's* the villain?"

I raise my hand, as if to say *It's okay, don't worry about it*- when it is really not okay, and I do hope she worries about it- before procuring a mess of garbled words, that are more grumblings of a madman than an actual, coherent thought. *"Ihh… mahh... zherna…"* And, again, drawing now from some untapped source of energy. "It's… my… journal…"

Her eyes widen at the realization-

His *journal? The journal I have been highlighting and dog-earing and devouring like a pre-teen on dystopian fiction…* His *journal?!*

-and that concoction of anger and shame becomes, overwhelmingly, diluted by shame (with bits of residual, anger flakes.)

"We need to call the police, like, *now*," Alexa says, pulling out her phone.

Dylan storms in, just in time to swipe the phone away. "No one's calling the cops," he declares jarringly.

"And why the fuck not?" Daisy questions. "If you're worried about me, if that's what it is, I don't give a fuck. I'll accept the consequences, whatever they are…" there is a sympathy in her eyes, "we just need to get this guy to a hospital."

An awkward, prolonged silence, before Dylan responds. "No. That's, uh… that's not the reason."

"Well, then what the fuck is it?" Alexa counters.

Serena and Dylan exchange glances. Dylan flicks his eyebrows, slightly, as if to say… *Your turn.*

"Your turn," I drone. "Your turn, Serena." It is quiet, and they ignore me. *Thank goodness.*

Serena is a contorted mess of warm, glowing colors as she steps forward, pandering to her housemates. "Look, I was going to tell you, but I didn't think it was that big of a deal."

"Didn't think *what* was that big of a deal?"

"The guys' house, they're worried about a narc, or something like that. I didn't get all the details. After the party, Dylan asked if he could bring the stash here, and…"

"You brought the stash here?!" Screaming, now. "You *bitch!* I'm going through withdrawals, I'm over here shaking and vomiting," and stabbing, you can't forget that one, "*and you brought that shit* here?!" Out of *all* places?

"Serena, Dylan," Alexa starts, palpable disappointment in her voice, "I told you already, I don't want any part of this. Dylan, you know the work she's putting in. You know how hard Daisy's trying to pay you back. And when she does, she's out, too. We've been over this." Dylan groans. "We've been over this, and, *you know what,* you should have known to ask us about this. Serena, that means you, too. But that doesn't matter anymore… what matters right now is that we get Forrest to a hospital. I don't care if your boyfriend's drug ring gets busted or whatever the fuck you think is going to happen, we are *calling* the cops."

Dylan smiles; I can't see it, but I can feel it. "That's sweet, Lex," he says menacingly. "Protecting your little crush, with the pineapple shirt, I get it… but, like I said…" he takes a step forward- *too* forward. His hand sinks into the crevice around her waist. "No one's. *Calling.* The cops," he finishes. "Serena, get your boyfriend over here. Cain will settle this, I'm sure…" His figure contorts wildly, like an inflatable, flailing in the wind. It is a motion that I can only assume comes from laughter. "The bastard always does, doesn't he?"

Chapter Two

Cain

Cain is extremely tall and extremely bald. He sports a black trench coat. I *think* he does, at least; at this point, it is hard to say what is real here, and what is fiction. His head shines like a beacon. A crown atop a towering, black lighthouse. He examines me, either as a hunter, assessing his kill, or a doctor, examining his patient. "You try pulling the knife out?" he questions, proving that he is, most definitely, not a doctor.

"You dumbass, that will only make it worse. We need to apply pressure… we need to get him to the hospital."

Cain raises his finger- *hush, hush*- waves it in a *nuh uh-uh,* sort of way. "We've got minds here, sweetie. And the internet. You put that all together," he smiles. "Nah… this kid don't need no doctor. Daisy-bud got him in the shoulder, nothing too serious. Nothing we can't handle." I can feel his breath on my face- warm, musky, and with a hint of whiskey- as his lighthouse beacon finds its way to the center of my burning photograph. "You're gonna' be just fine, kid, let me tell ya.'"

"*Yes, no, maybe so…*" I chant in a sing-songy voice, wearing that wide, shining smile that got me here in the first place.

He grimaces. "Seems to me that shock is as good a drug as any." He reaches into my pocket, and snatches my phone, before vanishing into the charred abyss of the photograph; there is a click of a gun. "Alright, I'm only gonna' ask this once. Everybody hand over your phones."

"You can't be serious."

"Serious as ever, Daisy-bud."

For most, not even a moment's hesitation. A soft *pat,* another *pat-*

"Dylan has mine."

-a *pat, pat,* and… the gun hangs in the center of the photograph. It hangs there for a considerable amount of time; except for this is not a gun, but the beak of a raven. An angel of death, guiding me to the other side.

The other side, which is either Edgar or the emptiness.

The gun fades away, followed swiftly by one, final *pat.*

"That wasn't too hard, now was it?"

Alexa's voice is wavering, but determined. "You're gonna' kill the kid. You know that, right?"

"Honey, I've got enough blood on my hands. You think I want more?" I don't know the guy, but I'm willing to bet the answer to that question is *Yes. If it works in my favor, most certainly yes.*

"Look, I don't understand what the big deal is," she continues. "We can get him to the hospital without bringing the cops over here. Just… if you would just let me take him to my car, I can drive him. I haven't had much to drink tonight, I could do it. Let me drive him."

There is a silence, which leads me to believe there is a deliberation. This doesn't surprise me; her proposal is reasonable enough. I know I've got a case of the *just-got-stabbed* brain, but I can't seem to think of a reason to deny it.

But he does. He denies it full swing.

There is a power in denying oneself. And maybe, for Cain, there is a power in denying others.

"Yeah, that's not gonna' happen, sweetheart." His words spill from his lips like venom. His arm, sheathed by that dreadful, black trench coat, slithers across my field of vision like a black mamba. Daisy's foot twitches anxiously, scathing my calf. "There are other forces at play here, if you know what I mean."

Daisy swats it away, as one would a gnat, and not a deadly, venomous serpent. "What the fuck is that supposed to mean, asshole?"

The mamba finds its way back to her shoulder, testing its boundaries. "It means that, if you're not careful, you may have a murder on your hands, little Daisy-bud. What happens when we call the cops then, my darling flower?"

"Cain," Serena hisses. "The *real* darling flower is back here, don't forget that."

"Sorry, darling." The mamba slinks away from Daisy's shoulder. I can't see it, but I can certainly hear it: Cain, the drug lord, wanders over to his girlfriend, gives her a peck on the forehead, "My mistake, my dove," before returning to the task at hand. "As I was saying... I *could* let you drive him to the hospital. But there are debts to be paid… *kingdoms* to be sustained, before I can allow that. Is that starting to make sense, Daisy-bud?"

It hasn't hit me until this, very moment: my life is on the line, and being debated before my very eyes.

"I don't have the money, Cain. I can get it to you… soon, I promise… but I don't have it yet. Take anything… I mean *anything* you want. It won't be enough, but I'll starve myself, I'll sleep on the streets, I don't care… I just don't want any blood on my hands."

The raven peeks its head out and plucks at Cain's glowing, white teeth. He gnaws on it, as a wearied child gnaws on the casing of a pencil. "Or… you *could* just… do what you do best, if you know what I mean. Return to your true calling, Daisy. That little Winter Wonderland… remember how fun that was? How *talented* you were at finding clients. Spinning that beautiful, white web…. No one did it quite like you. Remember that, Daisy-bud?"

"I wish I didn't."

"Come on, Daisy. Just one, little snort, that's all it will take. One snort and everything is back in order. You save a life, you avoid prison. And the best part? Your debts will be paid, in full. Provided you stay with us, that is. It could all be so… so *simple* Daisy. Doesn't that sound nice?"

Something lights aflame within me. A phoenix resurrected from the ashes. A courage I didn't know I had. My lips tremble, my tongue is quivering, but my words are clear: "Don't do it, Daisy. Not for me." If my death means freeing Daisy- Daisy, who brings me balance, like a river kissing a wildfire- then so be it. I will die, I will dine with Edgar and I will die if it means freeing her from that ghastly lighthouse and his Winter Wonderland.

There is a power in denying oneself.

The raven rears its head, and rests its beak between my eyes. "This is an A and B conversation, kid… you can C yourself out."

Yeah, but you won't kill me. You and your fucking lighthouse with your raven and your trench coat and your mamba... you are quite *a terror, but there's one thing I know: I am leverage, and you won't kill me. You won't fucking kill me because, while you may not be a doctor, you sure as hell aren't an idiot.* As a natural progression of that logic, I allow a glob of mucus, waiting patiently in that fringe world between the nose and the throat, to congregate, and form a menacing loogy behind my tongue. I send it catapulting out, freeing it from that dreaded cave I call my mouth. It is a pathetic spit- it peaks early and comes hurtling down into the crevice between my chest and neck- but the message is unmistakable: *you don't own me, asshole. C your own damn self out.*

The drug lord, king of Winter Wonderland, cackles maniacally, bending and twisting in a manner that seems quite unnatural for a lighthouse. "I like this kid, you guys. I *like* him." The raven flutters away. "I see what you saw in him, Lex, I truly do. And Daisy... oh... oh yes, I'm beginning to understand why you were so inclined to stab him."

"It's a shame," Dylan, Mister Dreadful, henchman to the lighthouse, chimes in, "he was a cool guy. Could have been a valuable member to our team, had things gone differently."

The mamba writhes around, finding solace, once again, in the valley that rests upon Daisy's shoulders.

"Still could go differently, Daisy. Still, very well could go differently."

The words hang in the air, suspended for some time, before, eventually, achieving their desired result. "I'll do it," Daisy says, succumbing to the silver tongue of the mamba. "Fucking manipulative demon asshole… I'll do it."

"Daisy…" I murmur. "Daisy, no."

That sympathetic look again. "Let's just get this over with."

Chapter Three

Diversion

I am alone, now.

They left me in here, bleeding out on the floor, while Daisy goes off to ruin her life, with a sniff of that vile, white powder.

There is a pattering. An ensemble of subtle footsteps which are, in fact, not that subtle. Alexa comes back into the room and crouches over me. "I'm going to get you out of here," she whispers. She has bandages. By the grace of God, she has bandages, and she wraps them around my arm in a way that I can only hope is the correct method. "Alright… that should be good, for now. But the hard part's coming, Forrest. I just need you to be ready. I need you to get up, and be ready." She pulls my un-stabbed arm over her shoulder and helps me back to my feet. "Lean on the dresser, and wait. Just wait. I'll come back to get you when it's time."

A drop of blood seeps out from beneath the bandage and lands upon the white, wooden dresser. A Japanese flag that quickly fades, as the red dot becomes a reddened Rorschach. *I don't know how much longer I can stand here.* The pain is agonizing; the world, along with my stomach, is churning like a madman. There is a clamminess… a hollowness within me. The sense that, if I fall to the floor again, I may simply shatter. And yet, even with that knowledge, I want to lay down. All I want is to lay down and dwindle away into the void. *The void, whatever is in that void…*

There is a rising babble coming from the kitchen- rising faster than the pace of my dripping blood- and it shows no signs of stopping. Something about loyalty. Something about Wonderland… she has a loyalty to Wonderland. She is lucky they are giving her a second chance, because of loyalty. Lex and Daisy, they are lucky. They are traitors, and they are lucky. It rises and rises and rises, until-

"If that's how you're gonna' play it… if you *really* want to talk about loyalty right now… well, I guess I'm just going to come out and say it." This is it. This is her diversion. This is how she gets me out of here. "*She slept with him, Cain.* Your little dove went and slept with Dylan. How about that for fucking loyalty?"

There is a reckoning. There is a backlash, but I don't have the energy to listen in on it. I keel over and nearly vomit. Nearly topple over onto the floor. I nearly shatter, but someone, *thank goodness,* someone comes to save me, in the nick of time. I was expecting Alexa- or Lex, whatever they are calling her now- to come for me, but it is not her. I knew it was not her, from the moment we touched. From the moment her hands swathed around my waist and the cold, clammy skin it is packaged in.

This is a river, wrapped around a sweltering fire.

Daisy's face, which only minutes ago had those fuming eyes and curled, maddened lips, presses against mine. Her hands, which crafted that silver branch in my shoulder, lock together and hold me in place.

There is a balance.

"Alexa sent me," she whispers. "It's okay, I'm going to get you out now. I started this mess. It seems only fair that I should end it, too."

Through all of this pain, I can't help but smile. It doesn't last long. "Did you do it?" I question. The most important question. "Did you give in… did you do it?"

"No," she says, and I believe her. "No, by some miracle, I got out of it."

"Alexa's diversion… it was a good one."

"Truth is always the best diversion," she is smirking, now. "Sometimes, you just have to wait for the right time to tell it." She brings me back into a (semi) natural, upright position. "Alright, we really have to go now." There is still shouting, which means we still have a chance.

"Go time," I say, starting the charge. Stumbling, slightly.

The house passes by as a dream. The hallway, which seems to tighten. Feels like the walls are closing in. The living room, where I spoke of Edgar and half-truths but dared not speak of that horrid night, all those years ago. The kitchen, where mamba and raven and lighthouse are entangled in a bewildering, black cobweb, with the beak kissing Serena's forehead, and then Dylan's. The mamba swooping in as back up, cradling the dove, and pointing accusingly at Alexa. The beacon shining every which way.

Then, the balcony, where those mesmerizing, swaying lights still hang. A view of the ocean and that striking, black horizon. The stairs, damp and wet and splintery. A rumbling beneath my feet, followed by the cold of the concrete *(am I barefoot? I guess I'm barefoot)*. That sweet, beautiful music, as Daisy, opens the door of her car and the engine revs up. "Are you good to-"

"I'm good to drive."

Dim, eerie street lights, flickering in the ocean mist. The strange emptiness of the freeway, followed by the lights of the city. A white building that gets closer and closer. It is not a tall building, by any means, but feels like it is towering over us, like a city in the clouds.

Daisy turns to me. "This is it," she says. "We made it." She gets out of the car, and helps me to do the same. A concerned nurse- I assume it is a nurse- sees us from inside, and starts running towards us. "Your journal..." Daisy says. "I just wanted to say thank you. You don't know how much your journal has helped me." Dog-ears and highlights and dystopian fiction... I had a hunch, but it is nice to hear it, straight from the river's mouth.

The river's mouth, which kisses me now, before placing me in the hands of medical professionals.

White, glaring lights.

But all feels black.

Chapter Four

Nate or Edgar?

I haven't journaled for a few days. Considering what happened to me on my last entry, I'm sure you can forgive me. There hasn't been much to journal, really. Several, bland days in the hospital. Recovering, and watching TV, mostly.

I healed up alright.

More than alright, if I am being honest. Sure, there is pain. There is the ache that comes with healing. But, coming so close to death really does foster an appreciation for life. I realized that, the moment I came out of the hospital. The spring air, it is sweeter. The sun, it is brighter. Music and dancing and friends. I'm kind of limited in the dancing department right now… but the energy. I still feel the energy. The colors- the green of the grass and the blue of the ocean- they have become more vibrant. The sound of waves, crashing on the bluffs. Over and over and over again.

Like Edgar, but beautiful.

I sit here now, wondering about the hope that pain brings. I sit here now, wondering if I really want this to end. Maybe, just maybe, I would be content as a wave, sliding across the sand, over and over and over again.

But there is more to be done. Edgar may be fading, but there is still some power to the thought of a natural, foregone conclusion. I have not reached that yet. Not by a long shot.

I go back to Rio, as an instinct but also as a search for that next chapter (which is, of course, one closer to the last).

Alexa is there, with the toucan perched on her shoulder and everything. She hugs me and makes sure I am alright. She gives me my phone and a pineapple smoothie, but not in nearly as bubbly a manner as she did on our first encounter. "I'm sorry I invited you to that mess," she says. There is a silent agreement not to speak any more about the incident.

On my phone, there is a text from a random number. *Hey, this is Daisy.* Okay, maybe not that random. *Alexa gave me your number, hope that's alright. Hope YOU'RE alright.* Then, in a separate text: *I think we need to talk.*

Yes. Yes, I think we do.

When we meet, her hair has been straightened, and is no longer frazzled. The swooping circles are hidden masterfully behind a layer of makeup. I can still see them, but only because I know what I am looking for.

"So, I'm guessing you're not pressing charges?" That's how she starts off; I get a good laugh out of that one, I really do.

"No, I'm not pressing charges. Did you really think I would have pressed charges?" After you drove me out of there? After that kiss?

"Crazier things have happened."

"Well, you're right about that, that's for sure." I take a sip of my diner coffee which is not quite as good as Rio coffee, but it gets the job done. "I think I just *experienced* one of those crazier things if I do say so myself." I gesture towards my injured, casted arm. "Which, while we're on the subject, could you explain to me what happened that night?"

"You don't remember?"

"I remember it fine, just have a lot of questions. For example…" I pull a crumbled, yellow list out from my pocket. "Ahh, here's a good one. Could you please explain why you stole my stuff? I have a pretty good idea, but, you know, I just don't feel like that's something we should leave unaddressed."

"Your 'pretty good idea' is probably right. I've been stealing shit to pay back Cain."

"And why, exactly, are you indebted to him?"

"Because I quit his little Winter Wonderland. And then I quit coke, to go with it. The way he sees it, I did him a disservice. On top of all the free coke I got for loyalty, he's making me pay for the future clients I could have gotten them… he's having me pay for the *potential cost of lost clients,* can you believe that?"

"Guy's a maniac, that's for sure."

"The good thing- alright well it's not *good,* per se, but it's not as bad as it could have been- is that he isn't making me do cocaine again. He just wants me to get him a couple more clients, and in return he said he'll lower the debt a little bit. Enough to where it's actually… well, feasible." She sighs. Or groans. I really can't tell which. "Alright, this is awkward, but it really is why I called you here: it's *feasible,* but only if you don't want your money back. I already sold your laptop, your headphones, and your watch." There is a twinge of grief about the watch. I never wore the thing- I have never enjoyed the feeling of passing time on my wrist- but it was a family heirloom. "So money is all I have. It's fine if you want it back, I'll give it to you, but…"

"In that case, you'll have to come up with a Plan B," I say, finishing her thought.

"Yeah, exactly."

"Keep the money, I don't want it. I only care about the journal. You can keep it for now, though, since it's helping you so much. Through the withdrawals, I'm assuming?" She nods. The beginning of my journal, the '*there is a power in denying oneself*' part of the journal, deals a lot with my struggles with withdrawal. From coke, too. Just like her.

"That journal was a godsend for me, Forrest, I don't know if you know that."

"You said something along those lines. At the hospital."

"And I meant it. You don't even know, Forrest; it's like I'm meeting my favorite author right now. Your journey was so... *mesmerizing*. And the courage you had... you knew you had to get off the coke, you *knew* it. I mean, I knew I had to, too... but you took *actual* action. That's really what got me off my feet, and off coke. When I read about your travels, when I read that you couldn't taper yourself off the stuff, so you flew to *Sweden,* and camped in the forest, alone, away from temptations..." And then I stayed there for three days, vomiting and quivering my brains out. I managed to lose the majority of my food on the second day. On the third, I ventured out of the forest to look for food, only to have a poor child ask if he could have any. "And then you gave him your entire meal. I couldn't believe that. I really couldn't believe that."

"Well, I meant it when I said it. There is a power in denying oneself. Even denying yourself food. It sounds crazy, but there's something about it. When you reject yourself, when you stop feeding into your desires, all of that inward energy is turned to the outside world. And there is a beauty in that."

"You went back into the forest, to find more of that beauty. And you fasted for three more days." There is a tingling, joyous feeling, just at the thought of that summer; that was, truly, the best time of my entire life.

It's a strange feeling, having someone relay your life back to you. But I adore her enthusiasm for those small details, some of which I have forgotten. Like the moose, who spent the night outside my tent. Or the whistling I heard one morning. I was sure it was human, but I never found the source. I enjoy her smile, as she tells these stories. It is nice to see her smile, despite the pain she is going through. I enjoy it, even, in spite of the pain she put *me* through. That smile is forgiveness enough for the silver branch she put in my shoulder. "And then that pastor found you, starving in the wilderness. He took you in and fed you. And he convinced you to visit the Holy Land..." And I flew to Israel. I went into the West Bank, into Bethlehem, and prayed at the spot where Jesus was born, "at the Church of Nativity." She eyes the silver cross necklace hung around my neck, and points at it, just as she did on the night of the Hot Seat. "The Church of Nativity, where you bought that necklace. Can I see it, again?" I pull it out from my shirt and hand it to her. It really is a simple design- just a cross and some beads- but she examines it carefully, flipping it over, swinging it, back and forth, in the light. "And then you went to Jerusalem, and went to the Holy Sepulcher, the spot of his crucifixion. And there, you bought another cross necklace. A wooden cross hung on a lanyard. And you converted to Christianity."

Her teeth glimmer in the fluorescent lights of the diner. She hands my necklace back to me. "That was a very important time in my life," I say, taking the necklace. "I'm glad I got to share it with you."

"Well, thank you for writing it. As I've said before, it saved me. It really did. And when I found out that *you,* the author of the journal that has done wonders for me… *you* were the one I stabbed," her eyes fall to the floor. "Forrest, you don't know how terrible I felt."

"Daisy, I don't want you to worry about that anymore. I didn't think it needed to be said, but I forgive you." I venture to the other side of the table and give her a hug. It lasts longer than anticipated. Not that I have any problems with that.

"Anyways," she says, taking a sip of her coffee, "I haven't read much past Jerusalem. I *just* started reading about your travels in France, but that's about it."

"That's a shame. You're about to get to the part where-" She nearly spits her coffee at the sound of it, and it takes me far too long to figure out why. "Sorry, I'll let you read that part yourself," I say, chuckling. "It is an indescribable feeling, to discover your life has become a spoiler." And she really *does* spit out her coffee at that one. "Should we talk about something else, then?" I ask, wiping the pool of coffee away with my napkin. "I've got a few more things on my list we could go through." I wave the muddled thing in the air. Wave it in Daisy's face a little, in hopes that she will, once again, spit out her coffee.

"Stop that," she says, giggling. But the giggling fades, and it is not long before the conversation returns to its serious nature. "Look, I was hoping we could be done with the subject, but I guess it is a fairly pressing matter." She places her hand on my wrist. "Do you think I should go through with the deal? It's lighter now, sure, but it's not great."

"Daisy…" I say, barely able to look her in the eyes, "you know, as well as I do, this new deal is not all it's made out to be."

"What do you mean?"

"What I *mean* is that, sure, right now it's just a few more clients, and you'll be in the clear. But you know he won't be finished with you after that. Probably won't be finished with you…" I scowl at the thought of it, "ever. Probably not ever." Then, another thought. And the scowl grows stronger. *A never-ending cycle of debt. Unless we do something about it, of course.*

"That's a bit extreme, don't you think? *Ever.*"

"Eternity is extreme. It is *the* extreme. That's why I'm so afraid of it." Edgar, seeping from the darkness, with his yellow, mangled teeth. "Sorry, back to my point-"

"No, screw your point. We can get back to your point." Something tells me that is not the case. Something tells me she knows what I am getting at, and it terrifies her. Taking a shot at Cain… that's just not something you do, is it? "I want to talk about *this,* right now. About Edgar. I thought it was just some joke, some bit you were playing to entertain us. You're telling me you're *actually* afraid of eternity?"

We've kind of veered off the deep end here, but, if that's where she wants to go, I'm all for it. "Of course I'm afraid of it," I say, diving in. "I know it seems weird, but think about it. *Really* try to wrap your mind around the concept of eternity. It's terrifying, isn't it? No end in sight, just on and on and on forever. Even just *thinking* about it, it can drive you mad, burns away at your soul. Can you picture it? In a million years, you have a million more to go. And a million after that. Can you conceptualize it? Where does the purpose go, after all that time? What is there left to drive us, after our storylines have burnt out? Do you think in a million years from now- a thousand, even- that there's anything worth living for?" A sting, almost a biting sensation, in my shoulder. I cringe, and my hand clings to the wound. Daisy reaches out and places her hand on top of mine. She rubs it gently. I know that won't do anything for it, but I appreciate it. There is a remedial, placebo-like effect to it. "Anyways, I'm ranting again, I'm sorry."

"I just don't understand it," she says, before releasing the wound.

"What don't you understand?"

"Well, think about it." She looks into my eyes, and there is a hint of guilt in them before she has even started. An attempt at saying, *This is going to be harsh, and I'm sorry, but I can't hold it in. There's something inside of me, Forrest, and I can't hold it in.* "Think about it, you actually *believe* in eternity. You have no reason to fear death, but now you're complaining the grave was defeated *too* harshly?" She slams her mug on the table. Whatever it is, something inside of her has taken over. "I *wish* I believed, let me tell you. I have my own fears, fears of the emptiness, which are much worse than Edgar." She goes into a squatting position, hovering above her seat and above the table. "A swirling vortex of nothingness, hiding beneath every footstep, peering around every corner, but only when you're not looking. Deadened eyes and heavy lungs that suck the energy from life itself." She smiles. "Let's call him Nate. He is all that, and yet he is nothing. All that power, and yet he is nothing. Can you picture it? One day, I may vanish. I may have left no mark on this world, whatsoever. Can you conceptualize it? Where is the purpose? What would be the point of existing in the first place? And sure, you can say all you want that the emptiness won't be that bad. We lived with Nate for eons before we were born, and that wasn't so bad, was it? And to that, I say, no. No, that is absolutely fucking wrong. You want to know why? Because life is like a drug; you don't know what you're missing until you try it. Life is a drug, and Nate is the withdrawal. The quivering legs and the vomiting and all of that shit I didn't have before my first whiff of snow, but sure as hell have afterward. The same goes for life, can't you see that?" She collapses onto the table; it seems that Nate has sucked the energy out of her, as well.

I place my hand on her shoulder, as a means of comforting her; she doesn't swat it away. "Nate or Edgar…" I say, droning off. "They're both pretty terrifying, aren't they?"

Chapter Five

The Point of Suffering

There isn't much talking after that.

I have barely scraped the surface of that crumbled, yellow list, but that doesn't bother me. There is something nice about the silence. We finish our brunch in peace and then pay the bill.

Climbing into Daisy's car, I notice she has yet to clean the blood stains. I come close to mentioning it but decide against it. Instead, I ask if she can drop me off at Church. It's a Sunday. There is a late service starting soon.

She asks if she can join me. *I* wish *I believed, let me tell you.*

I say of course she can.

I always find that they cover the more hard-hitting topics, whenever I bring guests. Maybe it is confirmation bias at work, but I have often considered the possibility that the pastor has some sort of sixth sense, and can foresee when the Church will be having an important, Sunday visitor.

Today, the topic is "The Point of Suffering."

The Church I go to is a modern one, and by that I mean it is held in a large, concert-like auditorium. They put that to good use, as they begin (and end) with what amounts to a Christian rock concert. There are several large screens, some displaying live lyrics, others with live video of the band on stage, and others with picturesque footage of beautiful scenery… mountains piercing the sky, fields of wheat, swaying in the wind. Waves crashing against the shore, over and over and over.

I have grown used to it over the years, and I always forget what an experience it can be for those who have never been. Daisy turns to me in disbelief as the woman in front of us raises her arms with a ferocity. Her eyes are watering, and, by the start of the chorus, that watering has transformed into a weeping. She screams *"Praise Jesus!"* and *"Lord, you are my LIGHT!"* between verses.

At this point, Daisy is enjoying it. She is singing with the music. Her eyes are watering, as well. It may sound like a madhouse, from the outside, but when you're *there,* it just makes sense. There is a feeling in the air. An energy so alive that the electrified woman feels almost natural. Daisy, eyes watering even with her disbelief, is par for the course.

It is *natural*, but it is by no means unremarkable.

Eventually, the band says their goodbyes. In the midst of this, the woman in front of us shouts *"Praise Jesus, my LIGHT!"* to which the lead singer responds, "Yes he is. In our darkened times, he is, most definitely, our light." He turns away from the mic, and the band walks off stage. Strangers embrace each other. There is a grown man with a tear streaming down his face. The music has faded, but there is an ambience in the room- a ringing in the ears and a ringing in the soul- and it is alive.

The large screens on the far right and the far left now display footage of the pastor, approaching the stage. The screen in the center has the topic for today- *The Point of Suffering*- in large, white font, atop a black background. "Wow, what a performance that was, am I right?" A wave of agreement from the congregation. "And Robby gave the perfect lead into my sermon. For Jesus is truly our light. Revelation 2:10 asks us not to fear our suffering, for if we are faithful until death, we will be granted the crown of life. If we follow that light, that goodness in our hearts, then we will be gifted that crown." The crown of life. Like Edgar, but beautiful. Golden points atop a crown, like the yellow, mangled teeth turned on its head. I have trouble wrapping my mind around it, but I am coming to appreciate the possibility. "While there is much suffering in this world, if we look for him, for that light… if we turn to the goodness of our *hearts,* ladies and gentlemen, and make certain not to return reviling with reviling… we may not put an end to all suffering, but we can certainly hope to minimize it. Please, if you would be so kind as to bow your heads, and join me in prayer today." Daisy is reluctant, but she bows her head and joins the pastor in prayer. "Lord, I pray that you soften the hearts of those that have joined us today, and are going through trials, as you went through your trials in the wilderness, and fasted for forty days and forty nights, and were tempted by the Devil. Lord, I pray that you guide me and my message today, as I tackle the question that has turned so many from you: if you are all-loving and all-powerful, God, then why is there suffering? I pray for those joining us for the first time today, and that they will hear your voice today, oh Lord, and find hope in the message I bring today. Thank you, Lord. Amen."

There is a shuffling as the entire auditorium leans back in their seats, and readjusts to the world of opened eyes and unbowed heads. "Let me begin by saying that there are, without a doubt, unjust sufferings. There are countless lives lost… lives of good people, lost. And there are awful, horrid people, who go on without a scratch. That is the state of the world, and it is undeniable. But every now and then, there is a light shown. A kindness, and a strength, that reminds us of the power in humanity. Some of you may scoff at the idea- and believe me, I understand it is a tough pill to swallow- but with each and every suffering, there is a purpose. Even in the case of unjust sufferings, there is a purpose. And that purpose is free will, ladies and gentlemen." Daisy does, in fact, scoff at the idea. She tries to hold it back, but that scoff remains as the pastor tells the story of Job, and how God allowed the Devil to test him. Could Job be truly righteous without a test? "He allowed it, as a means of silencing the Devil. He allowed it, too, because of free will. Because without free will, we would not have existence, as we know it. We would be mere robots. Puppets, in the hands of God. No, no, that is not the point of this world. That is not our purpose." He rolls his shoulders anxiously. He knows his words may be controversial. But they are true, and so he says them. "Like I said… it is a hard pill to swallow. But if God were to deny the Devil his darkness, how would we ever come to know the light? If God were to deny even the Devil his free will… what would become of this world? And if the light of God were not strong enough to withstand the Devil's test, then would God truly be all-powerful? This is a question that we, as humans, can only answer in the face of suffering. In the face of trials, and tribulations." Daisy squirms in her seat. She nearly gets up to leave, but something convinces her to stay. "Free will is the beginning of an answer, but it is not everything. We do not have the knowledge to answer this question. Not fully, at least. But I will begin to approach it- that weighing, gnawing question… *'What is the point of suffering?'*- by telling you what it is not. We do not suffer, and this I can promise you because God does not love us. John 3:16, you all know this one, I'm sure of it, 'For God so loved the world, that he gave his only begotten Son, that whosoever believeth in him should not perish, but have eternal life.' God went through suffering *himself* because he loves us. Ladies and gentleman, do you know of any author, who would voluntarily put himself through the sufferings of his characters? That is what the Lord did. Can you believe it? Surely, if there were no point to suffering, he would not put *himself* through it. Surely, our suffering is not because of a lack of love."

The sermon goes on, but for Daisy, it is over. I do not understand why now, of all times, but I understand there must be a reason to that squeeze of my hand, and the watering of her eyes, as she asks to pass through the aisle. I follow her without hesitation. I follow her outside, where she turns to me in front of an empty coffee stand with a rage and a confusion and a sadness on her face. "It's all a story, Forrest!" she screams. "All just one big, beautiful story!" A wailing, now. "I wish I could believe it, as you do, Forrest. The music, and the *feeling* in there, it's so beautiful. I *wish*

I could believe it, I really do. But it doesn't make any sense to me."

"Not everything makes sense to me either, Daisy. It doesn't have to. Why do you think I am a Christian when I am so afraid of eternity? Because I know that there are some things beyond my understanding. There are limits, and within those limits, I am terrified. But I believe there is a beauty outside of them, I really do."

"Your blind faith means nothing to me, Forrest. I'm sorry, but it doesn't. Not until you can answer this question: If he loves us, Forrest, if he loves us as it says in John 3:16, then why is there so much pain in the world? I know, I heard the sermon. I heard what he said. It's because of free will, and all that. But why can't he come down, and take our free will away, just for a moment? Just for the bad things? "What about my brother, a paraplegic, and with aphasia. Couldn't understand the Bible if you read it to him. Why couldn't he come down and save him before his accident? Why can't he come down, just for a moment, and put an end to the really bad things in life?"

I contemplate the question, but come up empty. All I can see is Edgar, with his mangled teeth. Turned on his head, it becomes a golden, shining crown. "And maybe the answer to that question is Edgar," I say involuntarily. "Maybe, in the end, the suffering doesn't matter. If we find the Lord, if we find Heaven- and I believe your brother can do that, even if he can't read the Bible- then what does it matter? What does death mean, when death is dead?" An image appears to me. An image of a sweltering fire, crackling in the hilltops. "Free will is like a forest fire, Daisy. Forest fires are natural, most of the time. Sometimes there are really bad ones. But even some of the bad ones are natural. And if you put them out, the forests become overgrown. The overgrowth, that's what you *really* want to watch out for. The overgrowth is what leads to the really, *really* bad fires. Fires that destroy ecosystems, instead of preserving them. If God came down and put out every forest fire, even some of the really bad ones, he would be doing us a disservice. And He can't put out fires altogether. He can't put out free will, Daisy. If He does that, then He denies our right to exist. Sometimes, Daisy, as awful as it sounds, you just have to let the fires burn out."

Chapter Six

Mister Dreadful's Plea

The drive home is silent.

This time, the silence is not so pleasant.

When we get to my apartment, she asks to come inside. "I can't go home, Forrest. What if Cain's there… what if he changed his mind? Please, could I stay at your place? Just for a little bit?"

I say of course she can.

It has been a tough day for her. Not as tough as the other night, but still tough. Heated, existential arguments. A thin but suffocating veil, pushing the threat at hand- the threat of Cain- into the shadows. It comes as no surprise to me when she plops onto my couch and buries herself in a mountain of pillows. I grab a blanket from my room, and drape it over her. It is not a particularly cold day but, for Californians, even a warm, summer day requires a blanket. I take a seat in the armchair next to her, and start to doze off myself. Drifting into that gorgeous, ethereal dreamscape. The sound of the world begins to fade, and swirl around some invisible, metaphysical drain.

That all comes to a standstill when, out of the corner of my eye, I spot a familiar figure making its way to my doorstep. *Well, that was nice while it lasted.* That excruciating noise as he pulls back the disheveled, screen door to my apartment; he takes a seat on a wooden stool in the corner, not bothering to ask for an invitation. Mister Dreadful, with those green-ish, grayish eyes. Those eyes which once ascertained my one, forbidden question, but now have a fear ingrained within them. "Hello again, Forrest." He turns to Daisy, who is still in a heap on the couch. "Hello again, Daisy. If you can hear me." She grunts, and that seems to be response enough.

"How did you find us?" I inquire, coming off not nearly as intimidating as I had hoped.

"Cain placed a tracker on Daisy's car a while back. In the front-right wheel well. You can check for yourself if you want." He shrugs. "I shouldn't be telling you that. Cain would be pissed if he found out. But he's pissed at me already, isn't he?"

"I'm sure he is. Doesn't really seem like the forgiving type. But hey, I just met the guy, so who am I to talk?" I roll my neck, and rub my temples with a vengeance, trying to force myself out of that *you-just-woke-me-up-from-a-nap* state. "Anyways, enough banter. Clearly, there's something you want. So- if you would be so kind- just spit it out already."

He looks towards Daisy, as if to say, *You may want to get off the couch for this one, Daisy-bud.* I reach over the armrest and tap her on the shoulder. She gets up, albeit reluctantly. "You were there that night," he says to her. "Forrest, you might not remember too well, but Daisy knows. Cain's gonna' kill me. Right now, I'm just on a hiatus from Winter Wonderland. But I'm no moron. I know what happens at the end of that damn hiatus. He's gonna' fucking kill me. He's gonna' fucking kill me for getting with his precious dove, I know he is." He moves from his stool, and places himself in front of us, on the coffee table. He leans in, getting dangerously close to Daisy's face. "You saw it too, didn't you?" She doesn't say anything, but that deadpan stare and that deadpan silence do the talking for her. He turns back to me. "I need to do something man, and quick. And not just *I*, but *we*..." his arms held out towards both of us, "because we *all* disrespected him that night. You, me, Daisy. You *know* that. You have to, don't you?" He whimpers. "You have to see that we're all in the same boat on this one. And it's sinking. I've seen how quick he works. I've seen how spiteful Cain can be. The boat is sinking, and it's sinking fast."

Daisy rises to her feet- a sense of fear and indignation rises with her- before wrapping a hand around one of Dylan's precious, matted locks. "Cain is a dangerous man, Dylan. You remember what happened to the last person that went against him?" She chuckles, and I wonder if that is a story I want to hear. "Hell, the other night… the bastard was going to let Forrest bleed out on the floor. He'd never met the guy before, but he was willing to let him die if it meant his debts were paid. This is not a guy you take a shot at and live to tell about it. The only escape is the long-con. Fade from his memory. Get out, while the time is right." She releases his dread, and he is quick to cradle it in his hand, as a mother cradles her child after a minor injury. "And the time is not right, Dylan. I thought it was, that's why I tried to leave… but it's not."

"And when *is* the right time, Daisy?" I can't help but agree with him, on that front. "There will never be a right time. You wanna' know why? Because that asshole is a master of Shock and Awe. Just when he feels that loyalty is fading… *wham.* You get the Forrest Night. You get guns pointed every which way. You get a kid bleeding out on the floor. And for what? It's a war on our will, Daisy, that's all it is. Just when the revolution is fueling up, he drains away at our will. *That's* why the revolution never happens. That's why there's only surrender, in our little Winter Wonderland… because of his damn Shock and Awe. And you know what? I'm tired of it."

Daisy examines him with suspicion. I can imagine there was a time when Cain and Mister Dreadful were one in the same. Equals- *equally* corrupt, *equally* nefarious- despite some key differences. Namely, who was head and who had hair on their head. I can imagine these are the thoughts running through her head as she dives into those ghastly, hybrid eyes. *You are not so innocent yourself, Mister. Unforgivable crimes, Mister. And now you come to me? Now you ask for my help?*

Apparently, such considerations are not strong enough to shatter Dreadful's argument: something now, or something never. Daisy's striking, hazel eyes find mine and ask for my take on the situation. She already knows the answer, but they ask anyway. "It was next on my list, Daisy, but I knew you didn't want to go there." I pull my torso over the armrest in an uncomfortable, almost kneeling position. "We need to put an end to Cain's treachery before it's too late."

"And how do you two expect to accomplish such a feat?"

"We could turn him in." A suggestion that is met with a howl of laughter from the more experienced in the business. "It's simple, I know. But what's stopping us? Surely, you two have evidence on him we could-"

"Let me stop you right there, bud. Cain might have seemed a little off the rails that night, but I can assure you, he is not an amateur. He is *very* good at covering his tracks. For one, he only allows spoken communication, so there's no paper trail, no digital trail. Come to think of it, I'm not sure he's ever touched the stuff. He always has others buy the product. Others move it, others sell it. He really is the brains of the operation, and... well, nothing else."

"But every now and then he comes barreling in with a gun. *Surely* he can't be completely clean." But, even as I say it, it dawns on me: other than vague threats from the raven, my life was the only one at stake that night. And for that, there was Daisy to blame.

"He's clean enough," Daisy says. "As clean as you or me, I'd say. But none of that matters. Even if we're wrong… even if there *is* something… there is not a doubt in my mind that he would find a way to kill us, before landing behind bars."

"She's right," Dylan chimes in. "If we're going to do this, we're going to have to think of something good. Something that will catch him off guard."

It's as if they think he is a god. A mighty, predatory bird, watching his kingdom from above, and ready to strike at any moment.

"Nothing catches him off guard, Dylan. Nothing."

But birds aren't all powerful. Birds can be caught off guard, just like the rest of us.

You know what we do to birds?

We put them in cages.

Chapter Seven

Daisy's Journal

Today, I figured I would get into the habit of journaling.

Forrest tells me it's a beautiful habit to acquire. It challenges you to appreciate the little moments. It helps to realize what went wrong in the day, and where it went right. And some days, when you are feeling nostalgic, you can just open your journal, and live a day over again. Unfortunately, there may not be many days left to relive. Forrest and Dylan have a plan if you can call it that.

I call it a death wish.

Of course, the guys are a little more optimistic about it. Today, we put the finishing touches on our plan of attack. It goes into effect tomorrow. So, assuming something goes wrong...

Yeah, this might be my final entry.

Whatever the case may be, I thought it would be nice to pay my brother, Eric, a visit. Forrest came, too. It was a nice drive. The view along the coast is always stunning. And, for the first time in... possibly ever... Forrest and I talked about something other than existential crises, or his journal, or Winter Wonderland. We just... talked. About how excited he was to meet my family. He asked what they were like, what it was like growing up with them. We had mutual road rage, and mutual admiration for that glowing, blue pearl we call the ocean, that always seemed to come out of nowhere, swooping suddenly over the guard rails of the freeway.

My brother and I used to live in the same town, attending the same school. He lives about an hour away, now, with my parents. It always breaks my heart, when I see him in that wheelchair. That dumb, cheeky smile on his face as he rolls towards me.

That smile dwindled, slightly, when he saw Forrest. He has never been one for strangers. Not since his accident, at least. After he saw the way we were with each other, how well he got along with our parents, and his extraordinary ability to make us laugh, I think he warmed up to him.

After dinner, my parents were cleaning the table. For a while, it was just me, Forrest, and Eric. I left to go to the bathroom, but I didn't go far and instead snuck and hid around the corner, to see how they interacted.

Forrest turned to him after about a minute of silence. "Eric, I have a gift for you. I know you can't understand me, but I have a hunch that you still have an appreciation for gifts." He pulled off his silver, cross necklace. I still don't believe in it- to me, it's still one, big, beautiful story- but, after joining Forrest at his Church, and our long, heated discussion outside of it, I am growing a deeper respect for it. So, when he handed that cross over to my brother, I understood the significance of the gesture. The silver cross, the one he found in Bethlehem, where Jesus was born. "I want you to have this, Eric. I did some bad, bad things… but this helped me. It helped me get my life together. It was a light in the darkness, for me. I'm hoping it can be for you, too."

Eric pulled me aside, later. He might not be able to understand language, but there is still a lot he understands. He pointed at Forrest, through the doorway, and looked at me with those longing eyes. He was asking a question, and I was pretty sure I knew what it was.

"Yes, Eric. I think I love him."

I've loved him ever since I read that damn journal.

Chapter Eight

This Could Be It

"I don't like your plan, Forrest."

I consider switching on the lamp, but I much prefer the sight of her face in the moonlight. *She's still here,* I think, and there is a glimmer of a smile on my face. When we got back to my place, after visiting her family, I never asked her to leave. I knew home was still a dangerous place, for her. I never asked her to leave, but she never asked to stay, either. I went to bed and figured if she was comfortable going home, she would. *But she stayed, Forrest. She stayed.*

"It's a good plan, Daisy." I throw my legs out from beneath the covers and swivel into a seated position. "And it's all we have."

"It's risky, Forrest."

"And so is not doing anything."

"I just don't understand how you can be so calm about it. You do realize if something goes wrong tomorrow… and something very well could go wrong… you do realize what that means, don't you?" Her hazel eyes amplify like blooming flowers. "This could be it, Forrest. This could be our last night, before…"

Before Nate, or Edgar.

I swivel back into my bed, making sure to lie on my good arm. Her hazel, budding eyes seem to bore into me, and if my other arm weren't in a cast or injured, I would have shielded my face from her radiance. "I think it's best not to think about that."

"And maybe you're wrong," she says.

Yes, I very well could be wrong about that.

It happens suddenly, but not unexpectedly; she lifts the covers and crawls into bed with me. I don't deny it; it feels… almost natural. *Natural, but not unremarkable.* "Are you okay with this?" she questions, and I nod my head. "Are you okay with… more?"

"I want to," I say, in an almost comatose state. "Believe me, I do. But I made a commitment." I reach for my silver, cross necklace, and am surprised to find my wooden one, instead. The one I got in Jerusalem, instead of Bethlehem.

"I understand," she says, wrapping her arms around me. "I like this, too." Wrapping her legs around me.

We stayed like that for the rest of the night.

* * *

Last night, cradled in her arms in the moonlight, was a thousand times better than anything I experienced. More than those three nights, long ago, before I turned away from the powder and turned towards the cross. Those nights were nothing, in comparison. Those nights were void of compassion and filled with lust. Last night was something else entirely. Something powerful. Something I have read about in books and seen in movies and heard in nostalgic grumblings from my parents and other happily, married couples, but had never truly *understood.*

There was one phrase that stuck out to me that night, above all others.

This could be it.

PART THREE

THE BIRD CAGE

Chapter One

And So It Begins

Pulsing music. Mesmerizing lights, swaying from the balcony.

My chest is the trunk of a black sedan, and my heart, its curious baggage. A ferocious desire to break free. The knowledge that, to struggle too much, is to risk everything.

The plan is simple. But it's risky.

I stand on the balcony above a trembling, reeling mob, like some mighty bird, watching over his kingdom. *But I am not the bird being caged today.*

Cain climbs up the stairway, his bald head reflecting the multitude of rays from the DJ station- green, purple, and red- like some sort of disco-lighthouse.

"And so it begins," Dylan whispers.

"And so it does."

Dylan stops Cain at the top of the stairway. "You remember Daisy's conditions. No guns, no weapons. I'm gonna' have to pat you down."

His arms shoot up like fireworks. "Frisk me up, buttercup," he says. "Wish you would have bought me dinner first." He smirks as Dreadful's hands make their way up his legs. "I'm curious, were you this forward with my girlfriend? Did you buy my girlfriend dinner, you know… before you fucked her?"

Dylan stares him dead in the eyes. It is not in his nature- as it is not in most people's nature- to go on without defending himself. But tonight, he will have to take the beating. *The knowledge that, to struggle too much, is to risk everything.* He gets back to patting.

"Submisive." he says. "I like it. Stay like that, and I may not have to punish you to the extent I planned." Dylan ignores the comment, turning to me, instead. He reveals a large bag filled with white powder, hidden in Cain's jacket pocket. *Looks like he* does *touch the product. Every now and then, at least.* He finishes the pat-down, and gives me a nod. Tonight will be raven-free, it seems.

The lighthouse turns its blinding beacon away from Dylan, and onto me. "Glad to see you've recovered," Cain says. "Hope there's no hard feelings, kid. Just business. You understand, don't you?"

"It's a cruel business. I understand."

He lurches towards me, snapping his teeth, and nearly chomping off a chunk of my nose. "You calling me cruel, kid?" *I think you know the answer to that one, lighthouse.* "I guess that's fair. I *did* let you bleed out for quite some time. And to be honest, it wasn't *all* business. There was a sprinkle of fun in there, too. That night was *terribly* fun, don't you think?"

He's just trying to get under your skin. Don't let him get to you. "I do like games," I say, trying to remain cryptic. "And that night was *quite* a game."

"Yes," Cain says, nodding in agreement. "It's all one, big, beautiful game, isn't it? And the most beautiful part? We're all players, whether we know it or not." The mambas he calls his arms coil around mine and Dylan's shoulders, as if we are reunited, childhood friends. That biting sensation in my shoulder returns with a vengeance; I would like to say my injury slipped his mind, but I have no such faith in Cain. "So, what are you two doing here, anyway? I've got to say, Dylan, I'm a little offended. Since when did you start working for Daisy, instead of me?" Dylan does not respond. Cain expected this, I'm sure. "And Forrest, as a fellow gamer, I have to know… what strategy, exactly, brought you to team up with the girl who stabbed you? Sounds kind of masochistic, if you ask me."

Daisy appears from around the corner. "They're not working for me, Cain. They're working for you.

The deal is for *you* after all, isn't it?" She smiles. "They're just helping me carry it out."

"I guess so," he says, releasing us. "I guess so." He slinks towards Daisy, and proceeds to massage her shoulders, those pronging, venomous fangs sinking into her tensed muscles. "How are you feeling today, Daisy-bud? Feel like stabbing anyone today?"

The disgust (and shock) on her face is imminent. "I guess we'll see where the night takes us," she says, playing into Cain's game.

"I do hope it takes us there, Daisy-bud. I really do. I was just telling Forrest over here, I quite enjoyed myself that night. Even if you *did* take the fun out of it, a little bit, when you drove him to the hospital." He sighs. "But that's alright. All is fair in love and war, as they say." Cain jumps backward excitedly, landing in a jumping-jack position. "Alright, let's get this show on the *road*. Where are these clients I have heard so much about?"

"Follow me," Daisy says, before leading him to a room around the corner.

The room.

The birdcage.

It is a simple room, longer than it is wide. It is a walk-in closet- rarely used, and with only a couple of jackets hanging- but we have made it look like a hallway. We spent this past week designing a fake doorway, on the far wall. "That door leads to a stairwell outside. I will invite the clients up, one by one. They'll come in here, make the purchase, and walk out the front door. No one will bat an eye." She eyes the fake doorway for a beat too long, before turning her attention back to Cain. "I'll get the first client, now."

"Yeah, go do that, Daisy-bud," he says, waving her off. "I'll be right here, waiting." He is eyeing the doorway, now. It wasn't the perfect job- the frame is slightly crooked, among other things- so I am not surprised that it has caught his attention. But we figured it was good enough. Good enough to get him in the cage, at least.

"Do you have the product?" Daisy asks Cain. He pulls it out, revealing, once again, that pouch of white powder. The goods of his precious Winter Wonderland.

Daisy backs out of the room cautiously; Cain's attention is still on that crooked, white doorway. Daisy's hand wraps around the handle, shaking anxiously. In those final moments, I catch a glimpse of Cain leering over his shoulder, his neck twisting like an owl, catching a glimpse of his approaching, nocturnal predator.

Daisy slams the door.

Dylan wastes no time, karate-kicking a large, wooden dresser at the snap of the door. It topples to the floor, just in front of the doorway. There is a loud crashing sound, barely audible over the obnoxious, techno-trance music, which has suddenly grown to an outrageous volume.

We've got him. We've got the bird in the cage.

I can't believe we actually did it.

"*What was that noise?!*" Cain shouts through the door. "*What the hell is going on?!*" The handle shakes maddeningly. Dylan pushes back against the dresser, which is rocking like a sailboat, braving a particularly vengeful storm. I rush to grab a pile of wooden planks from the bedroom. Daisy hands me an assortment of nails and a hammer.

"*The game's over, Cain!*" I howl over the music and the beating of my hammer. "*The police are coming soon! We've caught you red-handed!*" I nail the planks into an 'X' shape in front of the door. Daisy and Dylan have now returned with two, separate dressers. They place them, one in front of the other, against the original dresser, forming one, gigantic block, reaching from the doorway to the opposite wall of the hallway.

"*You haven't caught shit!*" Cain screeches.

Dylan pulls out his phone, opening up a live feed, streaming from the cameras we installed in the closet. We watch as Cain swings open the bogus door, revealing that same, pale-blue wall on the other side. "You assholes..." he says, speaking up again. "You haven't caught shit!" The mambas wrap around his temples, blocking out the blinding light of the beacon, and tighten their fangs with a ferocity. "*You're calling the cops on me, you morons?!*" He screeches. "*What is there to call about?! Tell me that... tell me why in the world you think they're going to arrest me!*"

Sirens can be heard in the distance, and the music responds in kind. Frustrated protests, calling for the party to go on, can be heard in the background.

"We've got video footage," Dylan says calmly. "We have footage of you with the product, Cain. Just accept it. It's over."

Cain falls backward onto the floor, cackling maniacally. "You and your crooked doorway and your barricade and your video footage... you have it *all* planned out, don't you? You think you're so... so *sly,* don't you? Well, riddle me this, geniuses... You think I would actually bring the product? The *real* product?!" He rolls over, slamming into the nearest wall. "This?!" he says, pulling out the bag. Searching for the camera. "Are you talking about *this?!*" He holds the bag up to one corner, although it is not the one with the camera. "This is just baking soda." He smiles. There is a twisted sense of victory in his laugh. He raises his finger- *hush, hush-* waves it in a *nuh uh-uh,* sort of way. "Daisy... my Daisy-bud... I expected more from you. Did you really think I was going to let you depart from this little Winter Wonderland so easily?"

Daisy presses her face against the door. "So what were you planning then, Cain?" she questions sternly. "Were you just going to sell baking soda to my clients? Because I have a hard time believing that."

"Of course not, Daisy-bud. I was going to give them a date and time for delivery. I was going to vet them myself after the fact… fuck, I might as well lay it all on the floor now. The plan was that *one* of your prestigious clients was going to turn up as a narc… and you'd owe me another debt, Daisy. You'd owe me another debt because you can never escape Winter Wonderland. You know that, Daisy. You know that."

Daisy's eyes widen. Those beautiful, hazel eyes. They shoot me a glance, enveloped in an emotion somewhere between fear and gratitude. *You were right. A never-ending cycle of debt.* But we took action. We stopped the wheel before it could start turning again.

Of course, putting an end to that cycle comes at a cost: the beginning of a new cycle. Something atrocious, certainly. But something *new*.

And so it begins.

Mister Dreadful reveals a raven of his own and presses its beak against the birdcage. "If that's true, Cain, if you *truly* don't have the stuff on you, then there's only one way I see this going."

Cain shows off a set of white, gleaming teeth to the camera (which he has finally found). "You gonna' shoot me, Dylan? Is that what's going on here? You gonna' shoot your dear, old friend? Because I can assure you, that is not a good idea."

"Seems like a fuckin' great idea to me."

I approach him, tap him on the shoulder, before mouthing: *No, Dylan. Don't do this.* He ignores me. There is hesitation, but he shoos me, and my plea for greater morals, away. "We were never supposed to kill him," I whisper, but he doesn't hear me.

Cain jumps up at the camera like an excited child. There is a shelf at the top of the wall, where the camera is mounted. He grasps the ledge of the shelf, and pulls himself towards the camera, making sure that his blinding, terrifying beacon is the only thing in view. "Dylan, pal, you can't shoot me. Why would you do that? The cops are on their way, right now. As it stands, you should already be taking off running, don't you think? You're trapping me in here for no good reason. There has to be some law you've broken by now, holding me against my will."

The siren sounds are getting closer, but Mister Dreadful seems undeterred. "I'd rather be in prison than dead, Cain. You live, and I'm as good as dead." Cain frowns and drops to the floor.

"Can't deny your logic there," he says.

"So I'm going to give you to the count of three."

"Dylan-"

"Three…" Cain dives to the floor, "Two…" he curls into a ball, pulling his knees to his face, "One…"

"Let me stop you right there." Another bird has fluttered onto the scene. Another bird, out of its cage. But this time, it isn't a raven, but a dove.

"Serena?" the lighthouse questions, his voice wavering. "Serena, is that you coming to save me? My precious dove?"

"Trust me, asshole, this is not for you." She smirks; I cannot see it, but I can feel it. "This is all for me, and I'm going to enjoy it every step of the way." She sifts her gun through a jungle of dreads and presses it to the back of Dylan's head. I notice a bundle of small, metallic pics, dangling from her gun-free hand. *She picked the lock,* I realize hauntingly. We were worried about unwelcome visitors, so we locked the doors. But she *picked the lock,* that sneaky little dove. *She's been following Daisy, with that tracker Dylan mentioned.* We removed it, of course. But not before her first visit to my house. *That's how she knew where I lived. And then she broke her way into the house.*

Serena, it seems, was indeed a force to be reckoned with.

"You can shoot Cain if you want, Dylan, I don't mind. You might miss, but I don't." She looks back at Daisy and me. "This was a mistake," she says. "You halfwits just ruined everything, don't you see that?"

"No, actually," I say, approaching her with confidence. "As a matter of fact, I have no idea what's happening right now. But I know one thing. You're not going to shoot him, Serena. Not on my watch."

"You think I won't?" she pulls the gun away from Dylan's head and begins to swivel it in my direction. Just at that moment, Dylan fires his gun at the ground, startling her. Her gun goes off, as well, the bullet penetrating the wall just to the right of my head.

Dylan tackles her and struggles for the gun. "Run!" he shouts. "Run, before it's too late!"

Chapter Two

Black and White

I take Daisy's hand and together, we sprint to the back of my apartment. There is a door there which *actually* has a stairway behind it, leading to a parking lot. "Where do we go now?" There is panic in my voice, rumbling as we make our way down the staircase.

"Alexa," Daisy says, panting for breath. "Alexa is at some sorority party, not far from here. She can help us."

We exit the parking lot and brace ourselves for the coming throngs of wandering, drunken students. People probably think we have gone mad, sprinting through the streets and the billowing, Friday night crowds. And, in a sense, we have. This night, which is certainly not even close to over, would be enough to drive anyone to the brink of insanity.

The party is only half a block away, and we make it there in good time. There is a bouncer at the front.

"Who do you know here?" he asks us, an infuriating question even when you are not being chased by a raving, trigger-happy force to be reckoned with.

"We know Alexa," Daisy says, still trying to catch her breath. "Please, we don't have much ti-"

"You're not wearing white," he says.

"What?!"

"You're not wearing white," he repeats. "The theme is black and white. Girls wear white, guys wear black. It was a pretty simple theme. You didn't get the memo?"

"Look, I don't care about your stupid theme. Please, just get Alexa, she can vouch for us. We need to get inside. There's someone-"

"Alright, alright, calm down. I'll get her, jeez. Just… wait here a second." He eyes me and my dark blue shirt, which very well could pass for black. "Is he your boyfriend?" he asks, seemingly out of nowhere.

"Yes, we're dating," she responds automatically. She turns to me once the bouncer walks away. "Sorry if that was a little forward. I thought it might help us get in."

I stand for a moment, frozen in shock, but in a good way. The ice eventually thaws, and a smile floats up from the chilled waters. "Don't apologize. We should…" It feels weird saying it. "Yeah, I like that. We're dating. Boyfriend and girlfriend." A Feng Shui to keep the peace. "If that's what you want… that's what *I* want…"

Those blooming eyes again, taken aback by how easy I was able to admit it. "Yes, that's what I want," she says softly. She stares into my eyes for quite a while, before going in, gingerly, for a kiss. It is short but passionate. It would have gone on longer if Alexa had not walked out at that very moment.

"Hey guys," she says, clearly hurt by the scene taking place in front of her. "You… uh… you want to come in? We can have some drinks in the house. It would be better if you were wearing black and white, but I think it'll be okay." Her voice seems to have had the energy sucked out of it, as if it has had a recent visit from Nate, and on a particularly parching day.

There is not much that we can say. Just guilty, warbling noises, as we struggle to come up with a proper response. "Yeah, that sounds nice," I say, eventually. "Thank you, Alexa." And then, in a measly attempt to cheer her up: "You wouldn't happen to have any pineapple smoothies?"

She smiles at me, but it is a sarcastic smile- *haha, funny!*- topped with an icy glare that pierces my soul. *Yeah, maybe I shouldn't have said that.* She leads us through a horde of cocaine white dresses, with splotches of Edgar-black attire. We get several awkward stares, probably because of our failure to comply with tonight's theme.

Alexa doesn't say another word until we are in the kitchen, where she pours three shots of vodka and plops them in front of us. "Hot Seat, anyone?" she quips, the energy slightly returning to her voice. There is a vague smile on her face, but it quickly fades to a frown.

"Yeah, I'll just go ahead and stab Forrest's other shoulder, while we're at it."

Alexa laughs politely, before downing her shot and walking away without a word. Daisy and I down ours soon after.

"Well, that was… unfortunate."

"You could say that again."

I shrug. "At least we're safe, now."

"For the time being, you mean?"

"Yeah. For the time being."

"I'm going to try talking to her," Daisy says.

"If you're up for it… yeah, that might be a good idea."

She rounds the corner, but must not have done a very good job at searching; Alexa comes out of the hallway not long after that, with a concerned look on her face.

"Are you okay, Alexa? I mean, I know, what you just saw… you're probably not okay… but-"

She topples onto the counter, and her face sinks into the cushion of her palms. Her eyes peek shyly through the slits of her fingers. Those emerald, green eyes that are usually so vibrant. Tonight, that vibrancy is gone; there is a pain within them that is haunting, and in stark contrast to the day I met her, with the pineapple smoothie and the toucan perched on her shoulder. "I'm sorry," she says simply.

"What are *you* sorry about? I should be the one apologizing if anything."

"No, not about that," she says, sighing. "I just don't want you to think I did it because of…" she walks away, refusing to face me as she says it, "Because of *that*."

"Alexa, what is going on?" But there is no need to answer. I can see the answer approaching; a dove, emerging from the sea of white.

"Daisy!" I scream. *"Daisy, she's coming! Serena is coming!"*

Daisy sprints down the hall, but it is too late. Serena has already pummeled through the door and is now pointing her gun in Daisy's direction. Seeing her at the last moment, Daisy is forced to an abrupt halt, and nearly trips over herself. She takes a moment to regain her balance. There is a wave of terror that surges across her face; fully grasping the situation at hand, her frightened eyes find mine. *"Get out of here, Forrest, while you still can!"*

Everything in my body tells me not to- I can't leave her, I can't possibly leave her- but my mind says otherwise. *If you allow yourself to be captured, you are both goners. Run, and you have a chance to save her.*

I make my decision.

At a moment's notice, I dive bomb behind the kitchen island, and slide across the tile towards the back, sliding glass door. "I'll come back, Daisy, I promise!"

"Oh, you'll come back alright," Serena says menacingly.

I bolt through the door, and into the backyard. Another narrowly avoided bullet; white, plastic shards shoot out from the threshold. One of them scathes my calf, sending a trickle of blood down my leg.

There is a short fence in the back. *You've got this, Forrest. You can do this*. I know it will be extremely painful, but pain, at this point, is the only option. It takes everything inside of me; fail-safes, revving up to their maximum potential. By some act of God, I mount the fence using only one arm, and my upper-body strength.

There is a jubilation, like blazing fireworks on the Fourth of July, as the jagged peak punctures my stomach. The joy recedes quickly, like a firework, dissipating into the night; the fail-safe gives out, and I find myself rag-dolling onto the concrete on the other side.

There is a ringing in my ears. The world is spinning around me, like a vortex. I want to give up.

I want to lay there, bleeding out on the sidewalk. The chaos can go on without me. I'm good, right here. Right where I am.

But you promised, Forrest. You promised her you would come back.

An image of a river, wrapped around a sweltering fire.

The fire crackles. It nips at the Earth and chars the soil. A fallen trunk makes a bridge across the river… and my sparking, puffing flames kiss the green on the other side.

The fire spreads, and I rise to my feet.

This is for you, Daisy. I smile, tottering forward, blood dripping onto the concrete. *I made a promise, and I intend to keep it.*

Chapter Three

The Skier

Friday nights here in this festive, college town can be dizzying in their own right. Parties are scattered throughout, and, much like spiders, there is always one close-by. The streetlights buzz overhead, in constant conversation with the drunk ramblings of the crowds beneath them: sometimes one or two cohorts, sometimes six or seven, melding together to form one, giant blob. Every now and then, one exceptionally intoxicated person begins shouting. Then there is that odd time you get a lunatic with an abhorrent desire to take a baseball bat to a side-view mirror.

Now imagine these same occurrences, but with blurred vision and a flustered mind. These same occurrences, popping around all at once, like popcorn or bubbles from a glass of premature champagne. This is what happens to me, as I hobble down the street, clenching onto my wounded shoulder, with a hint of red seeping through the sling.

I feel invisible, amidst all this chaos.

The smooth rattling of a bike chain comes to an abrupt stop and proves that I may, in fact, be invisible. The bike feels like a battering ram; before I can make sense of it, the ground rises from its natural position and greets me with a fist of asphalt. The tires roll over me, and its rider lands on top of me, elbows first, tearing into my ribcage.

At first, I think it is just a terrible accident. Some drunken biker who didn't see me coming, in my dark blue clothes. But there is no denying the leather gloves wrapped around my neck, and the infuriated, warm breaths coming from behind a black ski-mask; this is a targeted assault, no question about it. My eyes widen, and my arms flail around in some meager struggle, but there is no fighting this. Whatever *this* is, there is no defeating it on my own. Not with my bleeding arm and my muddled head and my splintered ribcage.

Fortunately, for me, one of the several cohorts passing by comes to my rescue, socking the skier in the face straight away. "Get off of him, man! What are you doing?!" My airways are suddenly free; I scoot back as best I can with one arm and a storm of pain surging through me, from my attacker and his vicious beat down. Whoever this guy is beneath the mask, he knows how to take a punch. Unfortunately, he knows how to evade them, too. Taking advantage of his attacker's wobbling arm, with his hand pressed flat out against the asphalt for balance, the skier kicks it out, grabs hold of his collar, and tosses the guy- who is by no means small- to the side.

Having defeated his assailant, the skier approaches me, with a sinister smile plastered upon the slit in his mask. "Who are you?" I question, lips quivering. And then, as if this is the more important question: "Why the mask?"

He presses his foot against my ribcage. "This is Winter Wonderland, Forrest, and I've come to ski."

The rest of the cohort rushes towards him but to no avail. He is a cunning skier and lunges to his bike before they can lay a hand on him.

"We can't let him get away," one grumbles.

"Yeah, you don't just strangle someone. You can't just toss Kenny to the side, and get away with it." He offers me a hand, and I would gladly accept it, if it weren't for the searing pain in my arms, stemming from even the *thought* of movement. "Are you okay, man? That guy got you good, dude. He got you real good."

Even speaking is painful; I wheeze in agony, as prongs of cracked ribs press against my lungs. "You don't have to tell me twice," I say. I force myself to laugh mentally, as I know physical laughter will be far too painful. "It hurts to move. Hurts to *exist*."

"Come on man, don't say that." He tries to lift me, but my body rejects it, snapping back to the ground like a refrigerator magnet. My senses give out; for a moment, there is only a numbness. A realization that I am, in fact, a bird, and this tattered body is the cage. *A numbness. You can use that to your advantage, Forrest. Come on. A promise is a promise.* My wings flap barbarously, trying to escape the cage. A hawk, with wings the speed of a hummingbird. The pain of the cage curled around my face, like orthodontic headgear… I understand that the pain *exists,* but I do not feel it at this point. I simply don't have the energy to feel it.

"Come on man, one more time. You can do it." He lifts me to my feet and, while there is a groaning, I do not reject it. One of the cohort places himself under my (slightly) better arm and assists me on the walk ahead.

"It's okay, we're gonna' find that asshole, and he's gonna' pay."

"*Yeah!*" they cheer in unison.

I appreciate the gesture, I really do, but vengeance is no longer on my register. I would have appreciated it more if they had offered to call the police or take me to the hospital. But that wouldn't have mattered in the end, anyway. If they had offered, I would have refused.

I have a promise to fulfill, before I can allow myself that privilege. All that is on my mind, right now, is finding Daisy, and rescuing her from Serena's clutches. *Where could they have gone?* I wonder. *Surely, they are not still at the sorority party. After the gunshots… no, they definitely booked it out of there.*

Upon second thought, this highly motivated cohort may work in my favor; assuming the skier works for Serena, finding him is probably the quickest way to find Daisy.

"He definitely went down this street, I swear I saw him," one of them says.

"Yeah, dude, I think you're right."

"Alright, man," the guy carrying me starts, "get ready to turn. It might hurt a little bit, but I think you've got it." We start to turn but are met with an aggressive, shouting drunkard, chucking stones at someone's house.

"You think you can just ignore me!" The drunkard screams. *"Let me in, you bitch!"*

Suddenly, that sound of clinking chains again; I flinch, and would have dived to the ground if my human cane didn't stop me. "You're okay, man. Just another biker." He zooms past us, the spokes reflecting the moonlight and the dim lighting of the street.

One member of the cohort, who seems to have acquired a taste for heroism, approaches the drunkard. "Hey man, I think you should probably go home. I don't know what's happening here, but you leave this house alone, okay?"

He pushes the guy. "Mind your own business, man."

"Excuse me?"

"Let me chuck my rocks in peace. These assholes deserve it." He chucks another one, shattering a window. *"Hah, take that!"*

"Listen," he knocks the stones out of his hand, "I'm not gonna' let this happen. You hear me?"

"Derek," one of them says, "I think we have other concerns ri-"

That soft, metallic humming. I dive to the ground for real this time. *"Dude!"* my cane shouts, "You can't just-" before realizing that this time is, in fact, the return of the skier. He whizzes past us, this time with a crowbar in hand. He swings at one of the guys, who ducks at the last possible moment. He dives forward, but the skier masterfully swerves around this tackle, before whacking him along the shoulder blades.

"Hey, rock guy," another shouts, "I found a *real* asshole for you."

The skier narrowly maintains his balance, and his crowbar. He cackles, before making a U-turn, and coming back for seconds.

"You're right," rock-guy says, scooping up a handful of stones. "This guy is prime target practice."

He tosses one of the rocks, but the skier bats it away with ease. It hits a nearby car, setting off the alarm. There is an aura of frustration that makes its way around rock-guy's face. "No one gets away from *me!*" he screeches, before chucking a stone into his spokes.

The skier loses control of his bike, and crashes to the ground.

"Get him!" several shout in unison, charging after him. Even my human cane charges ahead, leaving me to fend for myself. The skier abandons his bike and books it in the other direction. A stone-chucker, and a horde of fuming, vengeful frat bros, hooked on heroism, follow shortly behind him.

A make a slow return to the asphalt, landing graciously on my knees and one elbow. *A hawk…* I tell myself. *Orthodontic headgear… but you can't feel it. You don't have the energy to feel it.* My body may be a bird cage, but I am taking it with me. I stagger forward, eventually building a momentum that I can sustain.

"He came from the other way," I mutter to myself. "He got… the crowbar… from somewhere… over there." I make an erratic 180, and stumble in the other direction. *One foot… two foot… no, use the other foot you moron…. One foot, now the other…* I close my eyes, much preferring the inside of my eyelids to the chaos of the night. The raving music, the senseless shouting, the buzzing and the crying. *No, that's not smart. You have to look around. Find a house he might have gone to.* I must have found my way in front of yet another house party, as the music which I had hoped to block out is now at full blast, and breathing down my neck. My eyes flash open, revealing a yellow, orange-ish mess, with a hat of green.

A smashed pineapple, leaking out on the asphalt.

Chapter Four

Pineapple at the Gate

I follow the juicy river to the threshold of a driveway. The house, I realize, is strangely familiar. I follow the driveway to a small sidewalk, which leads to an open, wooden gate. I can no longer feel pain, but I can feel the rumbling of the music like no other.

There is no bouncer at this party; I walk in without a quarrel, other than the vague stare of a peculiar looking man, grinding on an attractive blonde. He pats her on the shoulder, as if to say, *I'll be back, don't go anywhere,* before leaving her, and walking intently in my direction.

Alexa, in her stunning, white dress, comes out of nowhere, intercepting the peculiar man's path. "He's okay, I've got him," she says, waving him off. There is a wide, anxious grin on her face. "I'm sorry," she says, the grin crumbling to more of a silent weeping. "I'm *so* sorry. I had to do it… I had to do it, but I shouldn't have." A meek chuckle. "You got the pineapple signal… I'm surprised that worked. *Really* surprised."

"Alexa, what is going on? Why are you helping Serena?"

"She's my best friend, Forrest. And she said, if I helped her, that she could put an end to all of this. Put an end to *Cain*." Frowning, now. "But I made a mistake. I didn't realize how far she was willing to go."

"And how far is that, exactly?"

There is terror in her eyes. "Follow me… you'll see, soon enough."

"Alexa, we need to get Daisy out of this. Dylan, too. Can you help us?"

"I can do my best. But, given the circumstances, I don't think my best will be very effective." She guides me away from the party, and to a secluded area behind the house, where the thumping of the speakers is replaced by a faint, hooligan-like chanting.

I swear I've been here before.

She leads me to a small staircase, where there is a small window with an ugly light shining through it, like an oozing, infected scab on ochre skin. On the other side is a throng of raving, shirtless men- and some women- many of which are sporting terrifying tattoos, such as black tear-drops leaking from their eyes, or roaring, mighty birds, made of only bone. There is a pit in the middle- a gouging wound in the center of a wooden floor- with dirt and rocks, and two weary inhabitants, with empty, wandering eyes.

Mister Lighthouse versus Mister Dreadful.

The fight of the century.

At the head of all of this is Serena, the menacing dove, standing proudly with a handful of hair in her hands. Hair which was once frazzled, and may soon be frazzled again, if it remains in this state for much longer. Daisy, crouched on her knees, hiding her horror as best as she can, but still shivering in fright at the monstrosity in front of her.

This is the new Bird Cage. This is the Dove's *Cage, and it is quite a sight.*

In her other hand, Serena wields a sharpened, shining scimitar, and raises it to the sky like Moses before parting the Red Sea. "The rules are simple," she says. "Only one of you lives." She tosses it into the pit. "Let the games begin."

Chapter Five

Becoming Cain

The Bird Cage failed, just as I expected.

We were close, though. We were close, but Cain brought baking soda instead of coke. Dylan threatened to kill him, but that all came to a close when Serena broke in.

Yeah, it turns out Serena- *I really can't believe it-* Serena *is the one we should have been watching out for. She is the* real *Cain and Cain was in fact just Abel who was to be betrayed and killed by his loved one.*

As of last night, I would say she achieved her goal.

Her goal of becoming Cain.

She took Dylan and Cain, but Forrest and I got away. We ran to Alexa… I trust Alexa, I really do. But last night that trust was misplaced. She claims it wasn't because of what happened (Forrest and I had an intimate moment, right in front of her) but no one can convince me that wasn't at least a part of the reason.

We ran to Alexa, for a safe-haven, and she turned us right back into the dove's wings. Forrest got away, but, with a gun pointed in my direction, I didn't have the luxury of running. I don't blame Forrest for that. In fact, I asked *him to run. I would have blamed him if he* hadn't.

Serena took me away, and, on the way to the next horrid house party, Serena told me all about her lovely goal of becoming Cain. "This is for your sake, Daisy, trust me." I kept silent. I wasn't going to let her bullshit get to me. "This is how we get Cain out of the equation, Daisy-bud." She even said Daisy-bud, can you believe it? "To put an end to your debts, we have to put an end to Cain. But we also have to earn the respect of all the deviants that bastard is tied to. There's only one way to do that, Daisy-bud, and that is to become *Cain. And who better to do that, than the woman who knows him best?"*

I hated to admit it, but, at that point, her plan was making a lot of sense.

Little did I know the senselessness it required.

"There is only one problem with that plan, and you know it as well as I do." She smiled. "That problem is my lack of a cock. You see, if I am truly to earn the respect of this tangled, snowy underworld… if I am truly *to become Cain… then I will need to put in three times the work as would be required from a man. I will truly need to become a force to be reckoned*

with," Forrest called her that once, and maybe I am misremembering, but I swear she said it, "someone no one will dare to mess with. I will need to put on a show for the masses. A spectacle, right here in Winter Wonderland. Today, Daisy-bud, we open our gates to this mass underworld, and we will not disappoint. Tonight will be a spectacle for all to see and remember."

We passed through a particularly scummy house-party, with odd looking men, much too old for this college town, grinding repulsively on attractive, young women who likely haven't placed their eyes on the heathens behind them.

She led me to a room in the back of the house, with an aggressive looking crowd, likely made up of the deviants, the other rulers of the underworld, she spoke of earlier. They were all lined up around a pit in the center. Two of the larger men in the room held Cain and Dylan on the edge of the deathly crater. Their eyes pled for mercy, crying out…

"Serena, why are you doing this? I am no threat to you… we were in the same boat, Serena. I don't know what we had, Serena… but it was special. *Couldn't you see that? It was special, and now you're just going to... throw it away like this?"*

"We had something, Dylan. But, to answer your question, yes. I am willing to throw it away."

"Weren't we in love, Serena? Serena, my dove, were we not in love?" Cain called out. "Before you fucked

my buddy over here, we were in love, were we not? Maybe you had something *with him... but ours... our* something was special... *that was* love, *was it not?"*

"Welcome to the spectacle, Daisy-bud," Serena whispered to me, before turning to Cain. "I asked myself that same question, Cain. I loved you. I did. But I am not so sure you reciprocated those feelings."

Cain snarled and shook like a circus tiger, held back by a precarious chain. "You're the one who cheated on me, Serena. You're *the victim here? Is that what you think, you manipulative, cheating..." the larger man wrapped his hand around his mouth. His eyes widened for a moment, and I can only suspect he bit the guy's palm.*

"Your time is over, Cain. It's that simple." Someone handed her a sword- a scimitar, I think- before she dragged me by the hair to the edge of the pit, my knees dragging along the splintered wood. She pointed the sword at the two larger men. "Unless, of course, you can survive the pit." She smirked, far too proud of herself for this comment. "Push them in," she commanded.

They landed face first in the stony, dirt-filled center. Puffs and clouds of dust seeped into the putrid air, causing several to sneeze. After wiping their noses, and a rumble of bless yous *throughout the room, the crowd roared maddeningly. Serena rose her scimitar into the air, as if to calm them.*

But there was no calming them. Not for this spectacle.

This spectacle begged for senselessness.

"The rules are simple," she shouted, before looking down at her two ex-lovers in the center. "Only one of you lives." She tossed the scimitar into the center. "Let the games begin."

Chapter Six

Mister Dreads versus the Lighthouse

"I have to do something," I say, trying at the door. Alexa pulls me back.

"You can't go in there, Forrest. She'll put you in the pit, too."

"Was that her plan all along? To have us all fight to the death?"

"I swear I didn't know, Forrest. I only knew that she wanted to replace Cain and get rid of him once and for all. I didn't know this is how she would go about it."

I don't think anyone could have expected this. Even as it unfolds before my eyes, I refuse to believe it. The scimitar clanks to the ground between Cain and Dylan. For a moment, they remain frozen. Staring blankly at each other. Unwilling to perform the act the entire crowd wants them to perform. I imagine, they were thinking back on that time, long ago, when they were actually friends. A time, maybe even before Winter Wonderland came along.

I'm sure those thoughts became more sinister, as the timeline progressed in their heads, and they were reminded of the fact that they shared a lover, who now watches over them, asking them to prove their superiority. The unfortunate memory that, despite their friendship, one of them had slept with the other's girlfriend, and had kept it a secret. The unfortunate memory that, had they not been thrown into this pit, one of them would have killed the other eventually.

They lunge forward, both in a desperate scramble for the scimitar, which results in a twisted game of tug of war. Dylan, unfortunately, grabbed the wrong end of the sword. While he managed to keep it flat in his hand and away from the sharp edge for a considerable amount of time, one, brisk jerk from Cain sent it slicing across his palm, and sending a spew of blood onto the dirt.

Cain takes a swing at his old friend. There is a loud, metallic whistling as it flies over Dylan's head, which ends up slicing off one of his dreads. Cain overshot, if only slightly, and his powerful swing has sent him tumbling to the side of the pit. Dylan takes advantage of this, and charges at the lighthouse. He knocks him to the ground. There is a large *THUD!* from the beacon as it knocks against a slightly larger stone in the dirt. A trickle of blood flows down his shining, white head as Dylan struggles for the scimitar in his hand. He takes hold of it, and it wavers, rumbling there for a while and scraping against yet another stone.

Cain releases one hand from the scimitar, and takes hold of the stone beneath his head. He raises it- Dylan's attention on the scimitar- and smashes it into the dreadlocked head of Dylan, his ex-best-friend. Dylan shudders, before thumping against the ground.

"Dylan, *no!*" Daisy shouts, her voice rising above the jubilated screams of the audience. Cain rolls Dylan over; there is still a bit of life in his eyes. He takes hold of the scimitar, and raises it above Dylan's chest. "Mister Dreads…" Daisy cries, using the nickname we have given him over this past week. A nickname which is dangerously close to his *actual* nickname, in my head, of Mister Dreadful. "Mister Dreads, *noooo…..*" She wails, her hand reaching out into the pit, and towards his likely unconscious body.

Maybe he was not so Dreadful, after all.

Cain turns to her, his eyes watering. There is a humor, but also a pain, in those eyes. "I'm sorry, Daisy-bud…" He turns away, and the scimitar pierces through Dylan's heart. Iron-red blood leaks out onto the dirt, like juice from a smashed pineapple. "…but Mister Dreads is now Mister Deads."

I have to hold it in, but I scream internally, pounding softly against the wall in agony. My shrieks, the pain burning within me, *all of it,* the curious baggage of a black sedan… to struggle too much, is to risk everything.

But soon, there will not be much to risk.

Chapter Seven

Dove

"A valiant effort, Cain," she says, clapping. "A valiant effort, indeed. And your prize? The right to life. For a little longer, at least." She tugs at Daisy's hair. "But I believe you will find your next competitor to be more of a challenge."

"Serena, my dove, please don't do this…"

"And why not?" Serena shouts. "I know the answer, Cain. I know what is going to happen, beyond a doubt, when I throw your precious Daisy-bud into this pit. The question is, are you willing to admit it? Or do I have to spell it out for you?"

"Serena, I don't know what you're talking about." He glances at his dead friend beneath him. Only now fully processing what he has done. He backs away in disgust.

"Tell me, Cain. This is your last and final chance."

He looks to Daisy. Looks deeply into her eyes. Then back to Serena, rage and sadness and power emanating from her all at once. "Serena..."

"You loved her!" she screeches. *"You always loved her!* I was only your second choice... but your precious Daisy-bud... she was always the one you loved. *I* was expendable, but she never was. Not in a million years."

"Serena," Daisy butts in, "that's just simply not-"

Cain cuts her off. "It's true, Daisy. I have to admit it at some point, don't I?" There is still blood dripping from his head. "I love you, Daisy-bud. I have always loved you." Daisy's face contorts in a mixture of confusion, distaste, and pity, with pity clearly overwhelming the other flavors.

"*That's* why I cheated on you, Cain. It was as clear as day to me, even though you would never admit it."

Cain howls in laughter now, rolling in the bloody soil. "You want to know something funny, my dove? Do you? You'll get a kick out of it, I'm sure."

"I have no time for your foolery, Cain. You have already made enough of a fool of yourself today."

"Oh... but this is a good one, my dovey-dove-dove. You want to know why I call you dove? Want to know where it came from, that lovely old name?" He jumps to his feet, and glares into his ex-lover's eyes. "Because you're right. *You're right,* I didn't love you. Not in the slightest. And I tried to fake it. I tried to say those words," he closes his eyes as he utters it, *"I love you.* I tried to say them, but I couldn't bring myself to do it. I tried to call you *my love,* but the words made me want to vomit." He holds his hands against his neck, and mimes a choking, gagging action. "I'm an honest guy, Serena, and I couldn't lie to you like that. I tried to say *my love,* but they only thing that came out was, *my dove.* Dove… short for *don't-love.*" His glaring white teeth reveal themselves once, more, but this time with specks of red splattered throughout. "Don't you think that's just… just so *funny,* my dove? My *don't-love, I-could-never-love-you.* Isn't that just *hilarious?"*

Serena squeals at a pitch so high, I worry I may go deaf at the sound of it. *"Yeah, that's some grade A comedy, you dipshit! How about this for your next bit?!"* In an intoxicating fit of rage, she releases Daisy's hair, and kicks her into the bloody, dusty, stony pit of death.

The prying against the latch is no longer constrained. The strikes against the panels are no longer silent, and can be heard, I'm sure, from miles away. The trunk breaks open, and the sedan comes to a screeching halt, chucking me onto the asphalt of life and death.

The crowd turns to the window, but a moment too late, for I have already broken free from Alexa's hesitant grasp, and bolted to the back of the house.

I remember this place now. I remember it in shockingly intricate detail that, even for a writer, I never knew I could produce.

I know how to get her out of this Bird Cage, and I am going to do everything in my power to do just that.

Chapter Eight

The Panel

Years ago, back before I came to Christ, and worshipped the white powder instead of the cross, I had a group of friends I didn't care for, other than their stash and their constant, friendly donations of snow. It's an era in my life that is foggy, and even if it wasn't, I would have tried to block it out all the same. But the power of pain can do wonders, and suddenly, that sketchy group of friends and the countless hours spent at their grimy house is coming back to me as clear as day.

When we would get especially high, we would always meander to the back of the house, where their gnarly (but exciting) death pit was. We would have our own little fight club, and beat the living daylights out of each other until there were no more lights to beat out.

I knew it. I knew this place was familiar. That death pit, with its dirt and its stones and its… I tried to block it out, I really did. The concussions and the coke surely helped with that endeavor.

On more than several occasions, even with the pain-killing quality of the coke, the aching would become so bad, I knew that I had to switch from fight to flight, and I had to do so without embarrassing myself in front of my powder-wealthy friends. Eventually, I discovered a loose panel at the back of the pit, beneath one of the spectating ledges. In those flight response moments, whenever my opponent would get distracted, I would kick out the panel, and usually manage to escape without a trace.

The coke surely helped with that endeavor, as well.

That panel, if I remember correctly, would lead to a window-well type of area, as if there was once a desire to build a basement, but it never came to fruition. A wavy, metallic wall, that, once traversed, brought you to the back of the house. But I don't remember a stairway there, meaning the panel must have been on the other side of the house.

Sure enough, on the other side, hiding carefully amongst the dying grass, is a small, metallic wall. There is only a small space to crawl through, and the walls- one wooden and one rusted metal- crush against my sides. *That makes sense. I was much skinnier back in my snorting days.*

And yet, I manage to squeeze through, despite the excruciating pain which is beginning to make itself known again. I slink into the dark, musky space, and fall to my back, probably resting next to some venomous spider, finding haven in the darkness.

This is it, Forrest. This is how you fulfill your promise. Everything in your life has led up to this moment.

I press my feet against the far wall, which I cannot see but I am fairly certain is the location of the broken panel. "It's loose," I say, a ray of hope shining within me as the wood wriggles beneath my feet. "The thing is loose… I think this is it. *This is definitely it.*"

I can hear Daisy's voice, muffling through the cracks of the panels. "Cain, you don't have to do this. *Please* don't do this."

Then, Serena. "Actually… he *does* have to do this. Or *you* have to do this, Daisy. Because if you don't," there is a cocking of a gun, "then Damien over here is going to shoot you both." I press my feet against the panel, and get ready to kick. "I'm giving you from the count of five." I pull my knees back, "Five…" I take a deep, inhaling breath, "Four…" I launch them forward, but it only shifts slightly. *Shoot, they must have fixed it up.* "Three…" I kick again and again and again and again… "Two…" Another deep breath. *You can do this, Forrest. You're the author of your own destiny, sure, but now you're the author of* Daisy's *destiny, as well.* I pull my knees in once more- one, final time… it has to be- and launch my feet into the panel with all of my might, every ounce of strength in my body coming to the forefront. "One..." The panel snaps in half, and the obnoxious light of the bird cage, the *Dove's* Cage, comes shining through.

In that last moment, I see Cain smiling, his treacherous, gleaming teeth shining for the last time, like the beacon of a lighthouse- this time, that smile is not so treacherous... it is kind, somehow- before plunging the scimitar into his own heart. "I love you, Daisy-bud... I always did." He collapses back against the corpse of his ex-friend, Mister Dreads who is not so dreadful. In his final, groveling words: "Just let her live, my dove. Just let my precious, Daisy-bud live."

Daisy crumbles to the bloody soil, writhing on her hands and knees. Serena is laughing, now. A monstrous laugh, in between heaving, weighing cries. "Yeah, that's not going to happen," she says with surprising clarity.

The sound of sirens can be heard in the distance.

"I wanted you to face off against Forrest, but it seems we are running out of time, and my associates failed to find him." She glares out into the crowd. "We can talk more about that later, but for now, I have other business to attend to. Richard, if you would be so kind... I would like to land the final blow." Richard, who must have been the one to cock the gun. Richard, who is likely traversing the room, to give his gun to his new leader, the Queen Dove, head of Winter Wonderland.

You only have a few moments.

"Daisy," I whisper, loud enough for her to hear, but hopefully quiet enough for her to be the only recipient. Her head perks up, but she probably thinks she is imaging it. *"Daisy!"* I say again. *"Right now!"* She turns to me, and the tears and eye-shadow streaming down her face are reminiscent of a river, carrying along a stream of charred earth. "I promised to get you out of here Daisy."

She lunges forward, her upper torso making it through the broken panel. I try to grab her arms, but the pain surging through me is now truly overwhelming, and I barely manage to make my way off of the ground. She thrashes around a bit-

"Where did the bitch go?!" Serena howls.

-she kicks several clouds of dirt behind her, before finally making her way through the splintered threshold. *"Forrest!"* she exclaims. "Forrest, how did you-"

"There's no time… I'm really broken up here Daisy… climb through... there's not much time. I'll go after you… just help me up."

She climbs over me- one of her knees presses into my cheek bone, but I do not mind- and into the window well, where she makes her way through the small exit in impressive time.

"She went through there!" someone shouts, pointing at the cracked panel.

Her face is like an angel, looking down on me from above as I drown in the darkness. She reaches down into the hole, and offers a hand, but all I can manage is a groan. "Don't do that, Forrest. You're the strongest person I know. You survived withdrawal. You fasted in the Swedish forest because of it. You survived when I stabbed you, and Forrest, I swear, you're going to survive this. I don't know what happened to you, or the price you paid to find your way back to me, but Forrest, I promise you- *this is my promise*- you are going to survive this."

The sound of sirens glares over our entire conversation. I can hear the crowd of drug lords- I assume they're drug lords- making their way into the pit, and towards the darkened cavern. Everything is closing in on us… just as the walls close in on me, as I manage to rise to my feet in an agonizing skirmish with my inner self, and Daisy pulls me through the small, enclosing crevice.

She yanks with a ferocity at my partially injured arm, run over by a bike tire, and it feels as if my body is going to be torn in half, but she keeps heaving. I can feel the grasp of someone's hand at my feet. Their sharp fingernails dig into my calf, and another hand grabs hold of my shoe. My shoe which comes flying off when, with one final yank from Daisy, my injured body catapults onto the straw-like, dying lawn.

We waste no time, and, even with my missing shoe and the pain wrapped around me like orthodontic headgear, we sprint away from that awful house, with its death pit and its fight club and its drug lords and its new take on the Bird Cage. We run and run and run, with red and blue lights glowing in the night sky, until we run into a familiar friend, who I have never met, but still know very well.

The Skier, with his vile crowbar.

"And where do you folks think you're going?" he says, swinging his dreadful weapon in the ocean mist.

"We're going as far away from this insane Winter Wonderland as we can," I say. "Ski as much as you want, but the powder is a little too red for my liking."

"Oh, Forrest… sometimes red snow is just part of the fun." He takes a swing of his crowbar, but not before he is taken to the ground by a police man. A legion of cops comes storming around the house-they seem to know the source of the deadly fight club-while several attend to the arrest of the mysterious crowbar-wielding skier.

"Are you okay, miss? Sir? Do you know what's going on here?"

"The only thing I know is that my boyfriend needs to get to a hospital, and as soon as possible."

The cop turns to me. "Is that right, sir? What happened?"

I try to muster a response, but can only smile. The world seems to sweep out from under me, and, for the second time in two weeks, everything goes black.

There are dreams of toucans and ravens and doves, pineapples (smashed and unsmashed), rivers and fires, Edgar and Nate… and the skier, that dreadful skier with his black mask cascading against ivory snow, which is sometimes red.

But, in the end, I wake up in the hospital with that smile still plastered on my face.

It feels blasphemous to smile in the face of such atrocities- Dylan's dead and Cain is dead… I even feel bad for Cain, with that kind grin and his sacrifice at the end- but I do because it's finallyover.

All of that pain is over, and now… maybe, just maybe… things will begin to move in the right direction.

PART FOUR

ANTEROGRADE

Chapter One

Forward

I always thought "happily ever after" was a load of crap. I always thought, after a while, it would become boring. A dull light fading into the darkness, but never fully fading.

I see now, that is not the case.

Happily ever after is a light which is powerful and lucid and joyous. A light which refuses to burn out, not because it is stubborn but because it would be unwise. Happily ever after is never written about in books because it is meaningless to everyone except the ones living it. A concept impossible to comprehend until you have become a part of it. In a way, life has become a constant, forward motion. Just like a shark that must always be swimming. This concept terrified me for the longest time- what if *I* were a shark; what if *I* had to keep moving… keep moving on forever, or die- but I realize now this is nothing to be scared of. The fear of this concept is built upon an inherent misunderstanding. A faulty cornerstone, if you will. I always thought the movement was the source of life, but, as it turns out, life is the source of the movement. I do not fear my need for breath because breath is not a thing I think about; it just *is*. The same goes for movement. The movement forward, in this glowing, vibrant life.

Like Edgar, but beautiful. Golden points atop a crown, like the yellow, mangled teeth turned on its head.

I didn't think it was possible, but, in my time with Daisy, ever since that fateful night in the Bird Cage, I think I have finally come around to the idea of eternity. I have found, and now understand, that mysterious *Happily Ever After.*

Not that everything is gumdrops and lollipops. The night of the Bird Cage broke me up pretty bad, physically and emotionally. The night of the Bird Cage brought about two funerals, one for our good friend, and one for our dearest enemy. There is always that dormant fear of Serena, that mighty, precious dove.

Serena got away. Most of the people in that abysmal house got away. I am pretty sure they captured the skier, but if I ever saw his face I wouldn't be able to identify him for the life of me.

Daisy moved in with me. She couldn't bear to live in the house where she stabbed me and got me into this mess. Not that the house of the bird cage, with that crooked doorway, is much better. Neither of us has mustered up the courage to take it down. It lingers there, popping up every now and again, reminding us of that unpleasant night.

I have a hunch that Daisy moved away, at least partially, because she couldn't bring herself to torture Alexa with her presence, now that we were dating. Alexa has been understanding, though. We hang out with her every now and again, and she supports our relationship.

The sleep-ins have been nice, but I think we are both hoping for something more. I think we both understand that this relationship is going somewhere more than just "boyfriend and girlfriend," which we so hesitantly agreed to at the front of that sorority party.

So it is time to move forward. It is time to follow the natural progression of life. I read somewhere that blood has a natural direction of motion. One set of veins brings blood towards the heart, while others bring it away. Antegrade or anterograde… something like that. Anything in the wrong direction- any retrograde blood flow- is dangerous and, much like a shark refusing to move, could prove deadly. Retrograde blood flow and motionless sharks, these things can *happen,* but they are a denial of nature itself. And while there is a power in denying oneself, the same does not go for denying nature.

There are only two roadblocks preventing this forward motion: a diamond and a question.

Make that *two* questions.

Daisy turned to me one night, during one of our many sleep-ins. There was concern in her eyes. "Forrest," she said, her voice soft above the sound of crashing waves coming through the window, "do you remember when we played Hot Seat?"

"How could I forget?"

"Yeah, no… I mean… of course you can't. But, do you remember…" She didn't have to finish. Something inside of me knew where this was going.

"That one, forbidden question? Is that what you are talking about?"

She nodded. "The worst thing you have ever done," she added, her voice barely audible.

There was a moment of trepidation, but it drifted. It drifted because I understood, in that moment, that I could not live a life with that secret buried beneath the surface; that would be a denial of nature itself. In order to move forward, to flow as blood in anterograde flow, one must answer the unanswered.

The thought of that night has always made me nauseous, but suddenly, I wanted to shout it from the rooftops. The sense that, if I could get this one, dirty secret off my chest, I could go on to live forever, and with a crown, instead of mangled, yellow teeth.

"Alright," I said simply.

"Really? You'll tell me?"

"Daisy, I might hate myself for that night. But my love for you..." that was the first time I had used it, that L-word. The first time I had spoken it aloud, even though we had both been thinking it. "My love for you supersedes that hate."

She rolled over, and hugged me gently. "I love you too, Forrest."

The sound of crashing waves, over and over again, filled that elongated silence before the story. *Hopefully, she still loves me after the story.* "One night, during my Freshman year," I started, gulping anxiously, "I was especially high on coke, not to mention especially drunk. But the coke... the coke I think is what really fueled it. I don't know if I told you this, but the reason I knew about that panel in the death pit was because I had a group of friends who used to live there. I'm not really sure how the hierarchy worked back then, but I am assuming it is before Cain rose to power, because they invited me to a party from the guy *they* claimed to be head honcho. I had been there on several occasions before that. At least, from what I can remember. That whole era of my life is overwhelmingly foggy... but I must have been there before, because I knew there was something wrong with the balcony. Someone had nearly fallen off... *something* happened, and I knew that one corner of the balcony was extremely flimsy.

"That bit of information proved to be… I guess you could say useful. It *wasn't* useful, not in the slightest; it led to the worst thing I have ever done. But in the moment it felt useful, I will say that much. It felt very useful, when one particularly aggressive attendant started berating me. Shouting hurtful things and tossing hurtful blows. I don't really remember what prompted his aggression. I don't really remember what he *said,* not to mention what he looked like.

"To me, I can only picture his face as that of Edgar's. Eventually, the fight made its way to the balcony. And you better believe I remembered that withered corner. When he threw another one of his punches, that I made sure to stand right in front of that corner. He had been overcompensating, and I was certain that, if I were to dodge one of his blows, it would send him stumbling forward. So that is what I did. I dodged him with a skill unwarranted for a man in my condition. And sure enough, he stumbled right into that brittle corner."

I stop to catch my breath. The memory of that night is far worse than I imagined. My insides feel like brittle soil, torn apart by livid corpses rising from their graves. Blood rushes forward. The shark speeds ahead.

"I didn't expect it to happen so quickly. It collapsed almost on impact, like an egg shattering against the side of a bowl. Splintered lesions of moldy wood rose like clawing hands, and this Edgar-looking guy fell into its writhing grasp, pulling him into the abyss. There was screaming. Shouting, in the depths of night. *Leave me! Leave me before I get my hands on you, you bastard! Leagghhhuaaaa....*"

Daisy gasped at the gory detail. I wish I could have held it back, wish I could have told it simply, wish I could have spared her... but this is yet another curse of the writer.

"I heard something snap, and there was more wailing. He was still crying out, still shouting, but it was horribly incoherent. A language I have never heard before.

"I scrambled back from the edge like an agitated crab, screaming all the while. The world around me seemed to spin around like a black emptiness, whirling and whirling. I ran back into the house, the foreign cries still booming in the distance. I didn't know what to do. Some part of me, the part of me overruled by drugs, convinced me that I couldn't save him. That if I were to go and help the guy, he would have killed me. He just fell off a ledge and probably took on some very serious injuries, but he could still kill me. *Save him and you die,* said the drugs. *Save him and you sink into that whirling blackness.* And, as my final, terrible act on that night- the worst thing I have ever done- I ran as far as I could. I ran without question. Several days later I woke up in a grimy motel, four hours up the coast. I don't know how long I was there. I don't know how I *got* there. I scoured through the news like a madman, let me tell you, but I couldn't find anything about anyone dying that night. *At least he didn't die,* I told myself, but that was a small comfort to know. There was something… someone was seriously injured that night. But it was several blocks away from the party, so that couldn't have been him. For a while I convinced myself the whole thing was a hallucination, but somewhere, deep inside of me, I knew it was real. And the fallen balcony, that was real. The drug lord told me as much, and I went back there myself just to confirm it. But they said they didn't find anyone in the wreckage. If someone fell with it, they must have gotten away." I groaned. I groaned in that awful, foreign language. "And that was it," I said. "That was the worst thing I have ever done. I promised myself, from that day forward, I would never do coke again. However, I did end up relapsing several times after that, and, after my third failure, I booked my flight to Sweden." I smile, but only because it's over. The memory of that gruesome night is over. "And… well, you know the rest of the story."

The confession was painful, but it was also refreshing. Like a skier, face-planting into white powder. Daisy's eyes watered like a swelling river.

There was an unnatural heat emanating from my body. A swelling river, wrapped around a sweltering fire.

She didn't say anything, she only wept. She wept for quite a while.

Eventually, it subsided.

"Daisy, can you still love me? Could you still possibly love me after what I've done?"

The waves made their presence known once more. "Yes, Forrest. Of course I love you." She said as I was fading to slumber. "It was an awful cowardly thing you did, but I still love you." She smiled, and hugged me tighter. My injured bones seemed to crack beneath her, but I paid no mind. "I love you because you told me."

I love her because she listened. Because she was able to give me a second chance, even after what I did. She loved me, even when I could not love myself.

A Feng Shui to keep the peace.

* * *

Daisy wants to return the money she got from stealing my bag. She doesn't have my laptop, my headphones, or my family's watch, but she has the money. She keeps telling me that. Keeps insisting that I take it back from her. She doesn't need it anymore, now that her debts have been cancelled.

This morning, I finally took her up on the offer.

As it turns out, my backpack and its contents were worth a grand total of $5,226. Apparently, my old, family keepsake watch was a lot more valuable than I imagined. The laptop sold for around $1000, the headphones just over $100… but the watch? I never wore the thing- I have always hated the ticking rhythm of time against my skin- but that watch was a whopping $4,100.

"Five-thousand-two-hundred-twenty-six dollars," I mutter in a sing-songy voice, snapping on my way out of the apartment. "That could buy a decent ring."

Chapter Two

Baptism

Things were awful in every way after the Bird Cage, except for what happened with us. *What I felt with Forrest… it was there before, but it grew to be as powerful as the sun. I cared for him, and his injuries. He would write for me, in return. He would write about how we were meant to be, how we were destined to find each other. He would read those passages to me before we fell asleep, like a children's bed time story.*

The day after Forrest's confession- the answer to that one forbidden question- we decided we should probably take down that crooked doorway, which is the ghastly face of the Bird Cage.

That morning, he took his money back. The money I stole from him. He had always been so stubborn about that money. Insisted that I keep it, even though I no longer needed it. I wondered for a moment what might have changed his mind, but after our use of the L-word last night, it didn't take much to put it all together.

It's an unfortunate thing, to know when a surprise is coming. You want to prepare for it; in the end, it boils down to nailing that "surprise face." Once that is perfected, everything works out the way it is supposed to. The surpriser feels accomplished, and the surprisee acquires the additional benefit of not looking like a fool. In the end, everyone wins.

I spent the day preparing that "surprise-face," among other things.

Later that night, we got to work on the doorway. I had a hunch his proposal would be related to the doorway. Call me Nostradamus, because that is exactly what happened. I went to pull that doorway back, and there, on the other side, was white, elegant handwriting atop baby blue paint.

Will you marry me? *it screamed in harsh, shrill tones.*

I switched on that surprised face I had worked so hard on, and clasped my hands to my face, gasping all the while. I turned around to find Forrest on one knee, holding an open, black box with a diamond for a tongue.

"Daisy," he started, his voice shaking anxiously, "not too long ago, we planned on making this room a Bird Cage. That night did not go as planned, not in the slightest, and I think I know why. Birds are meant

to be free, Daisy. Birds are meant to fly, and doors are supposed to lead somewhere. This beautiful, crooked door was once a dead end, but now it leads somewhere. It leads to a beautiful life ahead of us. I can see it, and I know you can, too. We may be young, but I know you can feel the balance… the chemistry we have together. That chemistry can last an eternity, Daisy, and when I am with you, I am no longer afraid of eternity. With you, I understand that the only direction in this world is forward. Would you do the honors of joining me, on this journey forward? Daisy, will you marry me?"

His eyes were watering and, even though I saw it coming, I couldn't hold back the waterworks, myself. My legs were shaking, my heart was racing. I felt like I was going to faint.

By some miracle, I remained on my feet. I should say that it felt *like a miracle, in that moment, but now I wish my legs had given in and I had buckled to the floor at that very instance. "Could you just… give me a moment?" I murmured between heaving breaths.*

"Of course, Daisy. Take all the time you need."

I made my way out of that horrid Bird Cage, and shut the door behind me.

As I told you, I spent the day preparing. And those preparations included keeping a large, wooden dresser outside of the closet. I knocked it to the ground without a moment's hesitation.

"Daisy?!" Forrest cried, worry in his voice. "Daisy, what are you doing?"

I brought out a set of wooden planks, and nailed them in an X-shape across the door. "Daisy, are you caging me?" His fist thrashed against the door. "Daisy, why are you doing this?!"

Forrest had his confession, and this is mine.

The worst thing I have ever done.

It starts with that one, forbidden question.

I should have never asked it.

And he gave me all the gory details, he really did. One night, a weekend night, during our Freshman Year. Before Cain came to power. When the old guy, Damien- it must have been Damien he was talking about- was in charge of things.

Oh boy, does that feel like a million years ago.

One night, Freshman year. Not long before he went to Sweden. Meaning it wasn't long before Cain came to power, and not long before I got myself involved in the business.

My brother, Eric, was a sophomore at the time. He knew Damien fairly well and would have certainly been invited to his party. (Eric was a cokehead, too, but now his pain medication seems to do the trick.)

And there was nothing in the news. Someone was severely injured that night, but that happened several blocks away. Surely, surely *that could not have been the case.*

But it was, Forrest. That was the news you were looking for, and you didn't even bother to investigate it.

Do you want to know what happened that night?

I had just made it to my friend's house, after a night of drinking. It had been a long night and was about to go longer. This was my older friend's house. A mutual friend of Eric's. He knew I was going to be there that night.

Thank goodness he did.

I was just beginning to socialize after an obligatory welcome-to-the-party shot, when Eric came stumbling in, hunched over and dripping with blood. He must have made his way, several blocks from that fragile balcony, bloodied and on the verge of death, to find me. There was a chorus of screaming, but Eric didn't seem to hear it. His eyes were glazed over. He seemed to be looking into some black chasm in the distance.

"Eric, what happened to you?! Who did this to you?"

And, in that horrible foreign language Forrest spoke of: "Aghdoonk nahhhll… Hockleeaaghhh maa… leagghhh…" Suddenly, clarity dribbled out from that treacherous void, strangling the whites of his eyes. He grasped my shoulders in one final burst of energy, leaving red handprints on my new, white blouse. "I love you, sis," he said, before his knees gave out, and his garbled body collapsed against the hardwood floor.

Those were the last words he ever spoke.

The day after Forrest's confession, in the time before his proposal, I paid another visit to my brother. I had to make sure this was right. If I was going to do this, I had to make sure it was really him.

I showed my brother a photo of him. His eyes grew wide in understanding. "Is this him, Eric? Is he the one who did this to you?" At first, he refused to answer. But his silence quickly transformed into a quivering, like mother's china cabinet at the first sign of an earthquake. "Is it him *Eric?! Is he the one?" I was crying at this point. Terrible, excruciating cries. "Tell me Eric... tell me! You have to tell me!"*

And that foreign language came back with a vengeance. I was certain his wheelchair was going to crumble beneath him, with all his ominous wobbling. "Hockleeaaghhh maa... LEAGGHHH!!!" he shouted ferociously, pounding his finger against the photograph, over and over again. Exhaustion gave in after a while; his head fell to the side, and he cried himself to sleep.

I tore the picture in half and chucked it to the floor. I stormed out of the house, with a fury in my heart. The Bird Cage may not have worked the first time around, but it was sure as hell going to work today.

And to think, when he told me that story, I managed to say I loved *him? Of course, I had been faking it. But at that point there was still a chance he was innocent. I don't think I could say those words, now. Would probably choke before I got to the L.*

And I thought, in that moment leaving my family's house, what if Forrest *choked? Wouldn't that be nice? Wouldn't that be much more pleasant, than a simple bullet through the doorway?*

Maybe I couldn't get him to choke. But I could make his death painful, all right. One for the ages, bet your money on it.

Another dresser, now. Just as we planned before. Dressers, lined all the way up from the door to the wall on the other side.

"Daisy, why are you doing this?!"

"You bastard," I shrieked, "You don't even know what you did. But that doesn't matter because you ruined everything, and now you're going to pay."

"Daisy-"

"You ruined my brother's life, you asshole! You tossed him off a balcony and left him to die! You took the words out of him, you bastard! You took the life out of him, and now you want to have a life together?! I think the fuck *not!"*

"Daisy, what are you talking about? Are you saying…" quickened, panicked breaths, "are you saying it was Eric? Eric is the one, I…" He was choking already. Choking like a fat man who refuses to chew. "Was it really him?!*" he wailed in agony.*

"Yes, it was him, you little shit! You ruined him, you ruined everything, *and now it's your turn."*

"Daisy… Daisy please. I didn't know! I have done everything, Daisy, everything I can to make up for that day! If you could only give me a second chance…. I… I loved *your brother! I gave him my cross, Daisy. Do you know how much that means to me?! I gave him my* cross! *I wanted to save him, Daisy… I wanted to save him." He groans arduously, and crashes to the floor, before erupting into hideous laughter. "Turns out, I was the one that needed saving, not him. It makes so much sense, Daisy…"*

"It's time to shut up now, Forrest. You don't deserve an epiphany. This is it, Forrest. This is how you-"

"Your brother's face… I always saw him as Edgar. Now it makes so much sense. I was afraid of eternity, because I never cleansed myself of that night. That night, *your* brother *was Edgar, all along. That awful, horrid night, that ruined your brother's life."*

"I don't give a shit about your Edgar and your fear of eternity, Forrest. My brother is not some character from your damn existential-nightmare-stories. My brother is real, *and what you did that night had* real *consequences." I sighed, and crouched in the corner against the wall. "You might not be afraid of eternity any more, Forrest. But you said it yourself: all stories burn out, at one point or another."*

"Daisy, what are you saying?"

I went to the kitchen, and grabbed a towering, white candle. I lit it, and placed it precariously on the ledge of a dresser, before walking away.

"Daisy!" *he moaned, battering against the doorway. "Daisy, where are you* going?!" *And, with all his brawling, he managed to knock the candle from the ledge. It fell to the floor, and the flames chewed into the carpet like a school of velvet-orange piranhas.*

"This is your burnout, Forrest."

A black fog filled the air, and a howling smoke-alarm whispered behind the clamor of the piranhas' magnificent, snapping jaws. I stood there, frozen and fascinated by its magnificence. It roared and curdled like a brilliant, beautiful beast, while it nearly swallowed me whole. I remember its warm embrace, hugging me like a mother hugs her child. It was a gleeful feeling, it really was. But I came to my senses and I made my way out of the house with a minor coughing fit. I stood on the street- crumbs of asphalt crunched beneath my feet because I was barefoot, was I really barefoot?- and I watched as the piranhas, which only seemed to grow, made a meal of the house where we made our first bird cage, and had our first sleep-in.

There were a lot of stories in that house. There were blank pages that could have been filled. White bits of tree, starving for black, oozing ink. But allowing such things would have been a disgrace; the shameful act of an author, who, as a betrayal to her art, has ignored its natural and foregone conclusion.

* * *

(Excerpt From Daisy's Baptism Speech)

"The majority of this book consists of entries from Forrest's journal. His *new* journal; the one he started after the night of the Hot Seat. Forrest let me read it when I moved in with him. Out of everything in that house, Forrest's journal was the one item I saved from the fire.

"I drove home that night. I wanted to see my brother. I wanted to hug him and tell him it was all over even though it wasn't really over. The pain he is going through may never end, but that's okay, I told myself. It is okay because Forrest is dead… an eye for an eye, Forrest is dead and everything will be gumdrops and lollipops from now on.

"As you have probably guessed, that was, most definitely, not the case.

"Eric was waiting for me. Sitting in his wheelchair with that dumb grin on his face when I stumbled through the doorway. For some reason he looked proud of himself.

"He had taped the picture of Forrest back together, and he held it up to my face along with Forrest's silver, cross necklace. He looked at me, hands writhing in agony, and spoke his first coherent sentence since the night he fell off that balcony.

"'I forgive him, sis,' he said excitedly. 'I forgive him, sis. I *forgive*.' He was waving it in my face, flicking it across my nose. The cold metal of the cross pressed against my face. 'I *forgive him,* see?'

"And he saw that I was crying, and he leaned forward and he hugged me.

"Forrest could never do it, but that day, my brother led me to Christ. He showed me that forgiveness and love are the two most powerful forces in this world… and if I had listened to those forces, instead of that potent song of vengeance, Forrest may still be here today.

"If the cross could bring even Eric to forgiveness, then maybe there was something to this whole Christianity thing.

"We went to Church the next week- the same Church that Forrest brought me to, the same Church where I met all of you- and I cried again. Even harder than the first time. I became a part of the community- this beautiful, loving community- and quickly learned where Forrest went wrong.

"Forrest never owned up to his mistakes. Not, at least, until it was too late.

"I would be a hypocrite if I never came forward. So, that is what I am doing now. Confessing my crimes to the world, before it is too late. It has been hard, building up the courage to make this book, but this community has helped. I have had a lot of support, and a lot of kind, loving words. With your help, and your kindness, I think I am finally ready to send this out into the world.

"I killed Forrest.

"I killed the man that I loved.

"I went through withdrawals from cocaine, and now I have withdrawals from Forrest, because even though he made a terrible mistake, I can forgive him. I can forgive him now because, with Christ, I am stronger. And, with that forgiveness, I can see Forrest for who he truly was. And I love that man with all my heart.

"But I will admit to you that I sought vengeance instead of forgiveness- I sought *fire* instead of *water*- and that is the worst thing I have ever done.

"I stand here today, with my feet in the sand and the waves crawling around my ankles, because I refuse to make the same mistake that Forrest did.

"I am ready to be baptized. And not just in water, but in the *ocean*. I want the world to swallow me whole and spit me out.

"So, world, do what you will to me. I only ask that you baptize me in water, instead of fire."

Made in the USA
Middletown, DE
14 March 2020